Witchy

'Witch . . . witch . . . duck her in the ditch! Roll her in the mud till she's black like pitch!'

Thrown out of home on suspicion of being a witch, twelve-year-old Aggie has to make her own way in the harsh world of the Fens in the 1890s. But wherever she goes, the gossip follows her, until she almost comes to believe it herself. 'If I got seeing and knowing,' she asks her gran, 'am I a witch?'

Befriended by the chapel-going Willetts, Aggie hopes she can put the past behind her and make a new life for herself; but then comes news from home and Aggie is thrust back into a life of superstition and hate . . .

ANN PHILLIPS was born in Ramsgate, in a house which was later hit by a bomb. She grew up mainly in Broadstairs and Stafford, and went to a girls' grammar school where she particularly enjoyed painting murals on the art-room walls. She went to St Hilda's College, Oxford, and read English, and then worked in publishing and college administration. She likes gardening, wild flowers, reading, going to church, and the theatre. *Witchy* is the fifth of her novels to be published by Oxford University Press.

Witchy

OTHER OXFORD FICTION

WITCHY

Ann Phillips

OXFORD
UNIVERSITY PRESS

OXFORD
UNIVERSITY PRESS

Great Clarendon Street, Oxford OX2 6DP

Oxford University Press is a department of the University of Oxford.
It furthers the University's objective of excellence in research, scholarship,
and education by publishing worldwide in

Oxford New York

Athens Auckland Bangkok Bogotá Buenos Aires Calcutta
Cape Town Chennai Dar es Salaam Delhi Florence Hong Kong Istanbul
Karachi Kuala Lumpur Madrid Melbourne Mexico City Mumbai
Nairobi Paris São Paulo Singapore Taipei Tokyo Toronto Warsaw

and associated companies in Berlin Ibadan

Oxford is a registered trade mark of Oxford University Press
in the UK and in certain other countries

British Library Cataloguing in Publication Data available

ISBN 0 19 275049 6

Typeset by AFS Image Setters Ltd, Glasgow
Printed in Great Britain by Cox & Wyman Ltd, Reading, Berks

ONE

'The witch is on the house! She's on the roof—she's up there!' Melia screamed; and even as she screamed there was a long undulating howl from above their heads, on the thatch, and a noise of scrabbling. The dog stood with the hair on his back bristling, staring at the fire. A lump of soot fell down the chimney and thudded into the burning peat.

'Ain't no witch,' said Sam, the middle child. 'Bowleses' old tom-cat—can't you tell?'

There was another howl from above, and Melia hurled herself at her mother, flinging her arms around her and hiding her eyes against the top flap of her mother's apron. (She's a big girl for that, thought Aggie, the eldest. She's eight; her chin comes over Mam's waist.)

Aggie looked at Dad for reassurance, but got none. Dad was a small man, and now he seemed smaller— shrunk into himself, huddled in fear. His eyes were turned unflickering on the hearth. Mam, Aggie saw, was looking at him, not towards the chimney. Mam's fears were always of the human, not the unearthly.

Aggie stood straight and did not mean to be afraid, but when the howling above rose to a screech she acted as if by instinct. She hauled the boots off her two feet, breaking the laces, pitched one of them straight into the fire, and heaved the other one out into the night as she snatched the house door open. 'Leave off, you danged old witch!' she bellowed. Sparks rose out of the fire.

There was a spitting and a slithering sound from above, something slid down the steep pitch of the thatch, and something shot off, rattling the bare bushes, into the dripping dark. The dog let off a volley of barks.

1

'Bowleses' old tom-cat, like I said,' said Sam. 'Listen to him go!'

'It were the witch!' sobbed Melia.

'Well, what were it, Aggie?' said Mam. 'You was the one knowed what to do.'

Aggie stood like a lump, her mind numb and confused. 'I didn't know, Mam,' she said. 'I just done it. I don't know nothing.'

But I do know some things, she thought. Things people do, and don't talk about. A child's shoe up the chimney, lodged on a sooty ledge, to keep a witch or devil from coming down; a man's boot buried under the doorsill to stop evil from coming in by the door. There were other things—she didn't know what, but she thought, bones—in the walls beneath windowsills to protect the windows from things trying to get in. Somebody in that house at some time had tried to seal good things in and bad things out. Or a builder had made magical protection to keep his work sound. It would be the same in the other houses of the village, and around.

Melia dried her eyes on Mam's apron, Sam shut the house door, and the people in the cottage seemed to come back to life. Even Dad straightened his shoulders and turned a sardonic stare on Aggie.

'And what are you wearing on your feet to school tomorrow, gal?' he demanded. 'You daft great gowk!'

Two

As might have been expected, the next day started badly. Melia woke Aggie by pulling her hair.

'Get up, Ag,' she said. 'Dad's got work for today, he's gone long ago. Mam's shouting for us. And what were up with you last night? You was moaning and grinding your teeth and rolling about, I near fell out on the floor.'

The two girls shared a bed in the stuffy small room; Sam slept on a folding bed set across the foot of theirs. Sometimes it folded in the night, with Sam in it, and the two girls tried to keep their helpless laughter below a screech—because if they waked Dad, in the next room, they would get a thump for it.

Aggie got up reluctantly, dragging on her blouse and her dark-blue skirt and tying her thick mane of black hair with a black ribbon. She and Sam took after their mother, tall and broad-shouldered and with heavy black eyebrows; Melia was like her father's mother, small-boned and slight, with mousy hair which curled naturally at the ends. Melia didn't need to make curls in her hair; Aggie had given up trying.

Aggie was disturbed by her restless night, by a headache, and by a vague sense that things weren't right. She doled the porridge Mam had made into bowls for the four of them, while Sam fed the dog Piper who was whining because he'd been left behind by Dad. The best spoon, which shone like silver even if it wasn't, had been put by Aggie's place when Melia laid the table. Aggie had no appetite, and sat playing with the spoon. She looked into the bowl of it, for the amusement of seeing her face reflected, queer and round and upside-down; she looked at the back of it to

3

see this distorted face the right way up. As she looked, she had the sensation of her eyes unfocusing; and then she was looking not at her own swollen face but at Mam's face, its proper shape but running with tears. She choked on her own breath and clutched the spoon against her chest.

Mam happened to see this as she turned from her stove with the boiling kettle for the tea. 'What's the matter, Aggie?' she asked.

'Nothing, Mam,' said Aggie, forcing out the words. 'I felt ill a minute. That's all.'

'She's had a seeing,' said quick-eyed Sam, always too observant for Aggie's comfort. 'She keeps doing it. Sometimes that's in the mirror, sometimes that's in the window when there's dark outside. Now it's spoons!'

'Be quiet, Sam,' said Mam; and Aggie simultaneously shouted at him, 'Hold your gab!'

'Well, it's true,' said Sam. 'She saw Bowleses' baby carried out of the water, the day before it were drowned.'

'It's no treat to me!' Aggie snapped at him. 'I felt sick all day after.'

'She's witchy,' said Melia complacently, gobbling porridge. 'Ag, if you ain't eating that, can I have it?'

'Eat it up, Aggie,' said Mam sharply. 'Now, Melia, and you, Sam. You ain't to talk about our Aggie's seeings. She can't help it happening, and it don't do no harm. Let her alone.'

'She can keep alone, for me,' said Melia, bouncing out of her chair. 'I ain't walking to school with her. She's witchy.'

'Get off, then,' said Mam. 'And don't call your sister names, or you won't get no dockey.' Dockey was their name for a packed lunch or a playtime nibble—bread and dripping, or cheese; and an apple if you were lucky.

'Can I wear me new boots?' demanded Melia.

4

'Aggie will have to wear those,' said Mam. And though Melia wheedled and wept, Mam stood firm. 'She's got one boot scorched almost through and one devil knows where,' said Mam. 'Of course Aggie must wear them. I'll go round the neighbours today and see if anyone's got a pair to spare near her size. And for now, get going.'

Melia ran off in tears and thundery glares; Sam went off after her, whistling. Mam put Aggie's dockey, a paper-wrapped bundle, into her hands, and held her arm for a minute on the doorstep.

'Don't talk to anyone about these seeings, Aggie,' she said. 'Or about last night. There's some sharp old tongues round here. And don't go calling Old Matty a witch, or letting the young ones do it. She don't ill-wish nobody, and people are glad enough to get their warts charmed or a herb tea for their bad stomachs.'

'I won't, Mam,' said Aggie; and she trailed away in the drizzling rain of early winter on the two-mile walk from Little Needham, her own village, to Fen Deeping, where the school was. She looked at Old Matty's cottage as she passed it—an even more run-down and shaky-looking one than theirs, with thatch tattered all round the edges like a mouldy mushroom. Bowleses' cat sat on the doorstep, obviously in the hope of a saucer of milk or a bacon rind. Old Matty, whom people called a witch and blamed for all sorts of minor accidents, had a very kind heart.

We're two of a kind, her and me, thought Aggie as she plodded by, her feet pinched by Melia's boots. We're the ones people are scared of.

The thought did nothing to improve her black mood. When Bob Fitch bounded out of his gate, with his usual greeting of 'Now then, Ag!', to join her on the path, he got a snappy answer—'Get off, Bob—you'll have me over!' Aggie knew she was nobody's favourite, today;

5

good humour and friendship were too much to cope with.

All the same, Bob's jokey company did make her feel the day might, possibly, get better. It didn't: it went all the way down to what Aggie felt was rock bottom.

THREE

Aggie was twelve, and the year was 1890; she was one of the oldest in the school. She could read, write, and add up—all after her own fashion—and knew a smattering of history and geography; by village standards, she was educated. She sat in a state of resigned boredom through lessons she had heard once before, and stitched a seam in which none of the stitches were as small as the 'carrot-seed' size required by the grim-faced teacher.

Playtime was dry and Aggie turned a rope for skipping and sang the rhymes. She didn't attempt to skip, in Melia's boots; but she still enjoyed the games. Her pleasure was dented when she noticed that Melia herself was not playing, but was in a huddle with her special friends Peggy and Sal. Aggie felt that these two looked at her oddly when the children went back into class: what had Melia been saying?

By the dinner-break heavy rain had set in, and the children ate their dockey indoors. There was one big classroom for the older pupils, with a single stove to heat it—lit now, as winter was setting in. Aggie, as a 'big girl', got a privileged place near the stove; she surreptitiously unlaced the tight boots under cover of her skirt, as she sat, and munched in comfort.

By now whispering and the slantwise looks seemed to have spread from Peggy and Sal to all corners of the room, even to the boys' side. Aggie felt sure the word 'witchy' came into it. In the confusion when the children were getting ready for lessons to begin again, Bob came over and gave her a playful punch on the arm.

'What you done, then, Ag?' he said. 'Frit the old witch off? Good job, I'd say. Couldn't do it if you

7

didn't have the power, though, could you, Ag? What'll you take to charm me pimples off?'

Bob certainly did have a nasty crop of pimples on his chin. Aggie looked at it with distaste, and gave him a push.

'Give over, Bob,' she said. 'I ain't got no power. That weren't ever a witch, that were Bowleses' cat.' She only half-believed this, but at least it made a plain straightforward tale.

'Your old granny had the power,' said Bob. 'She'd have made me pimples go, just like that. Come on, Ag, have a go.'

'Won't, then,' said Aggie.

She brooded through the rest of lessons about power (Was it the same as seeing? She didn't think so) and about the grandmother she hardly ever saw. Gran was Dad's mother, and Dad had fallen out with all his own relations and some of Mam's. Aggie was frightened by the thought that she had a power that she had never learned or asked for, and that she could not control. Her seeings were like that, involuntary, but they involved no action—they neither made things happen nor stopped them from happening. Thinking about seeings reminded her of the sight of her mother's face drenched in tears; her hands stopped working and her mind drifted.

'Stand up, Aggie Flack,' thundered the teacher, Miss Reeves. 'By my observation you haven't lifted a finger for five minutes or more. Are you in a dream, girl?'

'No, miss; I've got a headache, miss,' said Aggie, hoping against hope that she wouldn't get her knuckles rapped.

'That's no excuse for inattention,' said Miss Reeves. 'I shan't warn you again. Sit down and get on with your work.'

Aggie sighed with relief at her escape.

But the day's troubles were not over. She plodded home in the rain alone, even Bob Fitch not seeming to want her company; and not far behind her was a gang of boys and girls chanting,

'Witch . . . witch . . . duck her in the ditch!
Roll her in the mud till she's black like pitch!'

They never mentioned her name, but Aggie knew they meant her and she suspected that Melia was among them. The wet on her face when she got home came from tears as well as rain.

'Bustle around, Aggie,' said Mam at once as she got in. 'Lilian Bowles dropped me word as Dad's been laid off work and given his day's pay, so he'll be off to the pub. If he comes home with a skinful it'll be as well if you children have all had your tea and can clear off to bed.'

Aggie sensed her mother's tension. Dad was a holy terror when he was drunk; he usually took his bad temper out on Mam, but if the children got under his feet they could get a thumping too. He worked as a ditcher, maintaining the wide ditches or 'drains' which kept the fenland surrounding the village free from flood; and when there was no ditching to be done he would take farm work.

'Mam, is Gran a witch?' asked Aggie as she laid the table.

'Lord's sake, Aggie, of course she ain't,' said Mam. 'That's not to say she ain't got wisdom; she knows herbs and healings, and I won't swear she don't say a few charms. That's not being a witch, child, that's being a wise woman, that is, and it does no harm.'

'Old Matty then?' asked Aggie. 'Is she?'

'That's a bit different,' conceded Mam. 'But it's still wisdom rather than witchcraft, and there's no malice in her.'

Aggie said no more, as Melia and Sam came in wet and hungry. Melia was avoiding Aggie's eye.

It was late when Dad got in. Melia and Sam had gone up to bed; Aggie had lingered, wanting her mother's company. The cottage was tiny, with only one downstairs room. Heat for comfort and for cooking came from the peat-burning hearth at one end of the room; light came from a paraffin lamp with a tall glass chimney, which stood on the scrubbed table; water came from a well out in the garden, and the lavatory was a shack right down the garden past the gooseberry and currant bushes. But when the sun shone or when the lamp was lit the cottage was a cosy enough place.

After the young ones had gone to bed, and Dad's supper had been put to keep warm, Mam drank a cup of tea while Aggie darned her well-worn stockings. There was hardly enough money coming in to feed the family, at times; and never much over for clothes. Mam was a good needlewoman and did wonders with other people's cast-offs; but Dad would spend all the money she saved on drink—if he could get his hands on it.

'I got a bigger pair of boots, Aggie,' said Mam. 'I saw Carrie Bean in the street and I asked if she'd got an old pair going spare. Your feet and hers must be much of a size.'

'Oh, Mam, you're a marvel!' said Aggie. 'These ones are real pinchy. They'll be better for Melia.'

'Yes, if you ain't stretched them up to your size,' said Mam, and laughed. But her laughter died away in a quick gasp as she heard heavy steps on the path outside.

'He's back,' she said. 'Leave that work, Aggie, and get up to bed.'

'I'll stand by you, Mam, for once,' said Aggie. 'It shouldn't be always you to take the knocks.' She had no choice but to stand by, as Dad was in the room quicker than she or Mam had expected. He was plainly very

10

drunk. He left the house door open and stood swaying, hanging on to the back of a chair.

'You, Aggie,' he said in a loud growl. 'I want you out of this house.'

'Now, Noah,' said Mam placatingly. 'Sit down, do. Your meal's kept hot and there's a pot of tea made. Sit down and get warm; you look starved.'

'Not till she leaves this house,' said Dad. 'I don't want her here, so she goes.'

'But it's my home, Dad,' said Aggie, shocked and white. 'I ain't got nowhere else.'

'Not no more, it ain't your home,' said Dad. 'I say who lives here, and I say you go.'

'What have I done?' pleaded Aggie.

'What you done, it's the talk of the place,' said Dad. 'All round the pub and all round the village. Witchcraft, that's what you done. I won't have no witches here, and you're out.'

'But not now!' said Aggie. 'It's black night, and wet as hell. I'd die.'

'I warn you, Noah Flack,' said Mam. 'Turn a child out on a stormy night and you'll have the Rough Music round.'

Dad stalled. The Rough Music was something he did fear. It was made by neighbours, when they had finally lost patience with somebody's behaviour, coming in a crowd with saucepans and kettles—anything to make a din—and shouting outside the offender's house and ordering him or her to up sticks and go. Noah Flack, so unrelenting to his children and his wife, was afraid of what the neighbours said.

'She can wait till morning, then,' he said. 'But she can sleep in the pigsty. I won't have no dirty magic inside here.'

Mam came to Aggie and handed her her school coat, and Mam's own shawl. 'Best do as he says, Aggie,' she whispered. 'I'll creep out later and have a word.'

11

Aggie stumbled weeping into the garden, and felt her way to the disused pigsty. This was used for tools and stores; it was also where Piper, the mongrel dog (part spaniel, part mystery), spent the night. Aggie crouched on a potato-sack and cried into Piper's silky coat, and Piper leant against her, fanning up dust with his welcoming tail.

Four

Mam came as she promised, with a lantern in her hand and an old umbrella over her. Both of these stood by the house door, ready for people's trips to the privy after dark.

'Oh, child!' whispered Mam to Aggie, whose tears broke out afresh at receiving sympathy. 'Don't break your heart, child; it ain't the end of the world. Something like this were bound to happen. He's been on at me for some time, to send you off to work. He wants you out earning money and he wants a share of that.'

'It ain't that, Mam,' said Aggie. 'He says I'm a witch. You heard.'

'You know what I think about that, Aggie,' said Mam. 'I can't stay and talk now, or he'll be out after me like a roaring lion; I said I were only coming to the necessary. Here's a bite of bread for you, and here's the spare door key—he don't know I've got that, I had that cut secret because you don't never know, with him. When the light goes out downstairs, you creep back into the house and sleep where it's warm. I'll be down early in the morning and I'll have a plan.'

Aggie ate her bread, which had a scrape of lard on it, and gave a crumb or two to Piper; and when the light disappeared from the downstairs window she waited a while, then stole back to the house, let herself in, and curled up on the rag rug in front of the grate. There was still heat from the smouldering peat; and with Mam's shawl rolled up for a pillow, and all the coats the family owned spread over her, she lay and listened to Dad's snores from overhead. She would dearly have liked to sneak upstairs and into her own bed: but to get to the children's bedroom you had to go through Mam and Dad's (the house had no passageways) and this she didn't dare to try. Besides, Melia—being in such an unfriendly mood—couldn't be trusted not to give her away. Aggie made the best of things; and fell asleep.

Mam woke her, in the cold darkness of a chilly morning.

'Speak low, Aggie,' she murmured. 'Your dad has slept like a pig, but a noise might wake him now. I've packed up a bag for you, with your good dress and your smalls; and here's the boots I got off Carrie Bean. And I saved a few pence here and there, to see you fitted out when you left home; being as how I haven't had no chance to spend the money for you, it's all here in a purse. I got the purse for you, and all.'

It was a shabby, scuffed purse of black leather, but it had about two pounds in it in small change.

'How'd you ever get all this, Mam?' marvelled Aggie.

'I done a bit of sewing for people, and I never let on to your dad,' said Mam. 'He'd have had the money, else. I went to their houses to do it, so he never knew.'

'You're an angel, Mam,' said Aggie. 'But where can I go? What's to become of me?' She was buttoning her boots up as she talked. The 'new' boots were buttoned all the way up, no laces, and took an age to fasten.

'You're to go to Granny Flack,' said Mam. 'I thought we'd have time and I could look around for a place for you. But Gran will help: living like she does in town, she'll know where to try. You'd best be going sharpish: you can catch Bert Syme with his market cart, out on the road.'

'How shall I find Granny Flack? I don't know my way round that old town,' said Aggie.

'Ask for the Chapel Place almshouses,' said Mam. 'Anyone will tell you.'

Aggie's heart sank. If Gran was in an almshouse, where only the destitute went, she must now be too old

14

and too ill to help herself. How could she know about posts for young girls? She must be past it.

There was no time for goodbyes: a distant rumbling meant that Bert Syme's cart was on the road at the end of the cottage path. Aggie flung on her coat and hat, grabbed her purse and the old carpet-bag, gave Mam a hasty kiss, and ran for the road.

Bert Syme seemed pleased to have a fellow-traveller to Marksey, the nearest town. His candid smile and friendly manner suggested he had either heard no word of 'dirty magic', or didn't care: Aggie smiled back at him in happy relief.

She took a quick glance back at the cottage, hoping Mam might be waving at the door: but the door was closed already. A window upstairs flew open and Aggie feared to see her father's head come out; but what she saw was the blur of a small white face and lightish hair, and she guessed it was Melia. She turned away.

'Hop up the front with me, Aggie,' Bert said. 'Bleedin' dark, ain't it?'

Old Violet, his big black mare, plodded confidently under the lightening sky. Aggie watched as the flat, black landscape began to appear.

The Black Fens, she thought. Water and wet. Black magic. And I'm thrown out—

> Knocked out, socked out,
> Locked out of home—
> Chucked on the muckheap—
> Aggie alone . . .

The mare put her heavy feet down in a steady rhythm which matched Aggie's verse; and Aggie nodded, half asleep, until the Marksey rooftops came into view.

'Big old place,' she said to Bert Syme, beginning to be anxious about finding her grandmother.

'Not much more than a village,' said Bert scornfully.

15

'Norwich, now—that's the place. Cor, Aggie, you can't count the pubs in that place. Must be a hundred.'

'Marksey looks big enough to me,' said Aggie.

'Not frit, are you?' said Bert. 'Fine gal like you, you got the world at your feet.'

'Wishes ain't horses, Mr Syme,' said Aggie; but being called a fine girl had cheered her, and she went with a firm step into the market place and asked a friendly-looking market woman the way to Chapel Place. 'On up Market Street—left around Red Lion Hill—take the path past the school,' she chanted to herself as she went on her way. She had only vague memories of coming to town to visit Granny Flack (though she knew that Mam still sneaked in an occasional visit, under cover of going to market). Sam had been a baby when they last came as a family, she thought; and Gran had taken an afternoon off from her job as a cook in a pie shop.

A pie shop! thought Aggie. I could do that. Pity Dad had to go and have his row with Gran. Now then, left round Red Lion Hill . . .

Aggie followed the path beside the school, and was enchanted by what she saw at the end of it. A terrace of eight tiny houses stood in a half-circle, the space inside their curve filled with a slightly overgrown garden— seeding plants which must have had flowers earlier in the year, and plenty of bushes of various kinds. She recognized lavender, and hoped she would recognize rosemary. As she stood considering the bushes, a bucketful of water shot out of one of the little houses, hitting the shrubs beside her and spattering her with a sprinkle of droplets.

'Hey!' said Aggie involuntarily; and a white-capped head popped out from an open doorway to give her a saucy stare.

'Them as stands gawping gets a wetting,' said an even saucier voice.

FIVE

Aggie knew that voice, even after years; she thought she knew the small, sharp features too.

'Ain't you Mrs Flack?' she said, and getting a nod, exclaimed, 'It's me, Granny! What're you slopping water at me for?'

'I were giving them old bushes a taste of me dishwater,' said Granny Flack, grinning. 'And now I see you proper—well, it's Aggie, ain't it—me own Aggie! Cor, you ain't half like your mam, now you've growed a bit. Come along in, then, and see me little house. And tell me what you come for. News from your mam, is it? Something happened to your dad?'

'No, worse luck,' said Aggie, and then grew embarrassed and red. Dad was Gran's son, after all.

Gran gave a noisy hoot of laughter and tugged Aggie inside the little house—one near the middle of the row. Her walk was shuffling and slow.

'You can say what you think of that varmint,' she said to Aggie. 'Your mam would have had me along to live with you, when me legs got feeble; but he wouldn't have that, not he. Said it would cost him good money to feed me, and I were past work.'

'He ain't a kind man,' said Aggie sadly. At the same time she wondered wherever her family would have found space for a bed and chair for Gran, if Dad had welcomed her in. 'He threw me out, Gran,' she went on. She had to force the words out: but they had to be said sometime.

'What for, then?' asked Gran, as Aggie knew she would.

'I'm twelve, and he says I got to get work,' said Aggie. 'But it's worse than that. He says I'm a witch; and Bob Fitch at school says you're one, too, and I got the power off of you.'

'That you never did!' said Gran, and gave her brief, hooting laugh. 'Now sit yourself down, Aggie. Here's a pot of tea brewing and I'll toast you a muffin. Can you eat a muffin, child?'

Aggie didn't stop at one muffin; she ate two and Gran even found her an egg and boiled it in the pot hanging over the fire. Aggie sat at last full and contented, sipping strong tea.

'So tell me,' she said anxiously to Gran. 'Have you got power, Gran; can you charm off pimples?'

'Not charm, no,' said Gran. 'I ain't got power, Aggie; I got knowledge. I know the herbs, see. I know what leaf makes lotion for sore eyes and what's good for wheezy chests. But that's only knowing. There's seeing, now. I ain't got that.'

'I got seeing,' said Aggie. 'But I never asked for it. And night before last, we thought the old witch were up on our roof; and I knew what to do, and I done it. So that's knowing, ain't it? But I didn't know I knew. I never tried to know.'

'That comes out of your bones, that does,' said Gran. 'Anybody might know that.'

'If I got seeing and knowing,' persisted Aggie, 'am I a witch?'

'That don't sound like real knowing,' said Gran. 'So I say, you ain't.'

Aggie sat warm and comforted. 'Whatever I am, I got to get on,' she said at last. 'Can you help me to a place, Gran? A maid, or helping a cook?'

'I'll put me thinking-cap on,' said Gran.

'I'll need me uniform, won't I?' said Aggie. 'A black dress and an apron.'

'We'll look in me press,' said Gran. 'It's odds we'll find something.'

Gran's press was a tall, handsome cupboard against one wall of the room, which was crowded with furniture.

'How come you live here?' asked Aggie as Gran fumbled through the stuff in the drawers.

'Chapel people built these houses for widows,' said Gran. 'I'm chapel, not church like your mam. I got a bedroom, up them stairs; but I can't get up there no more—me old legs won't climb. I sleep in me chair, by the fire. You can borrow me bed, but that's three nights only. Chapel people made that a rule.'

She turned her head sharply at a chattering of children as they passed the almshouses.

'School's over,' she said. 'Now, Aggie, you run to the school and ask Miss Marriott—that's the teacher—if she knows of a place for a girl. She hears of places, on account of she knows what girls have left school.'

'Oh no—I couldn't!' exclaimed Aggie.

'Off you go,' said Gran.

Six

The teacher who answered Aggie's timid knock at the school door was a complete surprise to her. First of all, she was young—quite unlike Miss Reeves the knuckle-rapper. Second, she was wearing a paint-splashed apron. And third, her mouth was full and she held a bitten apple in her hand.

'Well, lassie?' she said. 'Have you come with a message for me?'

Aggie stood completely tongue-tied. Miss Marriott gave her an encouraging smile.

'Or are you a new pupil?' she said. 'You look tall, to be still at school.'

'No, I've left, miss,' said Aggie. 'I'm twelve. I've come to me granny—that's Mrs Flack—for help to find a place; and she sent me to ask you if you know of anywhere. It seems bold of me, miss; but me gran said, ask.'

'Always ask,' agreed Miss Marriott. 'Come along in, then, lassie. I know Mrs Flack, of course; we both go to chapel. And is your name Flack, too?'

They went into her house, which was tacked on to one end of the school building, and through a rather bare sitting-room to the little kitchen.

'For a start,' said Miss Marriott, 'suppose I give you dinner?'

Miss Marriott's dinner was a hot-pot in a brown crock, simmering on the hob. They didn't get a lot of meat each, but the potatoes and onions were plentiful and a slice of bread sopped up the good gravy. As they ate, Aggie told Miss Marriott about the school in Fen Deeping.

'Now tell me about yourself, Aggie,' said Miss Marriott when they finished. 'First of all, what's Aggie short for?'

Aggie was stumped. She knew Melia's full name was Amelia, though nobody but Miss Reeves ever called her that. But she herself was never anything but Aggie.

'It will probably be Agnes,' said Miss Marriott. 'We'll assume it's that. Well, Agnes! What are you good at? Do you like reading?'

'Not much, miss,' confessed Aggie. 'But then, I never had no interesting books. I like poetry, though; I make that up.'

'Oh, do you?' said Miss Marriott. 'Say me some.'

Aggie launched into her current masterpiece.

> 'Knocked out, socked out,
> Locked out of home—'

Miss Marriott's face was a mixture of dismay, laughter, and reproof.

'I'd call that a rhyme, Agnes,' she said. 'Didn't you learn any real poetry at your old school?'

Aggie racked her brains.

'"I wandered lonely as a cloud", now,' said Miss Marriott. 'Didn't your teacher ever read you that?'

'Well, she did, miss; but I never got beyond the first line,' said Aggie. 'A lonesome cloud! Did you ever set eyes on a lonesome cloud? Where I live they come in great flocks and herds, one after another. And if that's only one, then that's covering the sky. I don't see as how that can be lonesome.'

Miss Marriott laughed outright. 'You have an original cast of mind,' she said. 'But think on, Agnes. Couldn't you be lonely in a crowd?'

Aggie allowed that, and felt she had not come well out of the conversation.

'I know I'm not clever, miss,' she said sadly. 'I'm too

much of a country girl to work in a posh place, and I ain't got no brains. I could work in a kitchen, though. I could learn that.'

'I wouldn't agree that you haven't got brains,' said Miss Marriott. 'But I wonder whether your school showed you how to make the best of them. Did you enjoy school? Did you dream the time away? Were you scared of your teacher?'

Aggie had never had a chance before to talk about herself to a sympathetic adult, other than Mam and Gran. She was surprised by what she said.

'I don't know as I dreamed, miss,' she said. 'Nor I weren't specially scared of Miss Reeves. I were always scared of something, though. Me dad, and a bit of me mam when Dad had worked her up, and of meself. Of being a witch,' she explained.

'That's nonsense!' exclaimed Miss Marriott. 'Witchcraft comes by consent. If you don't want it, you won't get it. Nobody else can wish it on you.'

'But that runs in families,' said Aggie, desperate for the truth to be heard and reassurance, if possible, given. 'Gran had her kind of power—that's knowledge; I got my kind of power too. I get seeings, miss; and them seeings come true. What am I to do?'

'You must pray about it,' said Miss Marriott. 'And come to chapel with me. A good power drives out a bad one. You know that.'

'I didn't know that,' said Aggie. 'Who says so?'

'Everybody says so—even the devil himself,' said Miss Marriott. 'As for finding you a place, I shall ask around. I believe Mrs Lamb up at Lamb Place wants a kitchenmaid. I'll make sure.'

'Won't your own girls who've left want that?' asked Aggie, anxious to be fair.

'They're all suited,' said Miss Marriott. 'I'll give you a message at your grandmother's. Or in the chapel.'

Aggie dawdled her way back to Gran's, pausing to look at the yellow-brick chapel beyond the almshouses. It was a plain, unattractive building with heavy wooden doors and the name *Ebenezer* on a block of stone above the entrance. Aggie wondered vaguely why a chapel should have a boy's name.

She found Gran busily at work turning up the skirt of a black dress out of her cupboard, using the dress Aggie had brought with her as a pattern.

'I do believe this'll fit you, when I've done with it,' Gran said by way of a greeting. 'You was a long time with Miss Marriott—did you get your dinner?'

'Yes, stew with good meat in it,' said Aggie. 'Not chewy gobbets like you sometimes get. She's looking around for a place for me. She's nice.'

'She should be, she goes to chapel,' said Gran. 'I reckon you ought to go to chapel tonight.'

'She said that. But we're church,' Aggie objected.

'Ah,' said Gran. 'And do you ever go? You'll be the ones the vicar wishes Merry Christmas to when you come for Harvest Festival. Chapel ain't like church, Aggie. Thing is, chapel folk look after each other. Wednesday night, prayer meeting, seven o'clock. You be there!'

'Cor, blast!' said Aggie. 'I don't want to go, Gran. I'd be frit.'

'Ain't no good thinking like that,' said Gran. 'We're all frit of summat. You can't spend all your life scared to pieces that there's somebody under the bed. It's win or bust, Aggie.'

Aggie slid into her own thoughts. Mam was frightened of Dad; Dad, she thought, was frightened of other people. Sam was afraid of the dark, and of ghosts. She herself, she realized, was afraid of herself. And Melia? A horrible thought struck Aggie. Was Melia afraid of her elder sister?

'Gran,' she said, in a pause in Gran's flow of talk. 'Is Melia frit of me?'

'How should I know that?' said Gran. 'She might be jealous of you, though.'

'Her?' said Aggie. 'But she's pretty, Gran, and people like her. Even Dad likes her. He don't like me.'

'And if your mam is extra kind to you, to make up for your dad, Melia would cotton on to the kindness and not to the reason,' said Gran.

'You're real clever, Gran,' said Aggie. 'I like being with you. I don't want to go to no chapel, though.'

All the same she was at the door of *Ebenezer* at five to seven, shaking in Carrie Bean's boots. Somebody coming up behind pushed her inside—and into amazement.

SEVEN

Her rare churchgoing had not prepared Aggie for the experience of chapel.

The room into which she burst, shunted along by the people behind, was the hottest she had ever been in. It was about the size of a schoolroom, and had at one side a coke-burning stove which belted out heat like a miniature volcano. It was also as noisy as a schoolroom. It was packed with about forty hot adults and ten children, all talking.

'Take a seat, me dear,' said a well-rounded woman with a red and shiny face. ''Ave a 'ymnbook. And if yer cold, get up by the 'eat.'

Aggie went and sat by the least alarming people there—two little girls, the elder a bit younger than herself, who were there with a pale, neat mother. Aggie had hardly caught sight of these girls before she passionately envied their clothes and their looks. They had smooth brown hair in long pigtails and grey wool dresses with white collars; their boots were brown, not dreary black, and they had blue coats folded under their chairs. They seemed to be too shy to speak to Aggie, but their mother did.

'Are you a visitor to Marksey?' she asked Aggie kindly.

'Yes, ma'am,' said Aggie. 'Visiting my granny, Mrs Flack.'

'You're very welcome here,' said the pale woman. 'We know your grandmother, of course. Our name is Osgood; my girls here are Hester and Miriam.'

'I'm Aggie Flack,' said Aggie. And to the girls, 'Do you go to the school here?'

'No,' said the elder girl, timidly. 'We don't live in town. We live in Hardingley. There's a school where we live.'

Aggie was opening her mouth to ask where Hardingley was when a commotion at the front suggested that things were about to happen. A hymn was announced, and the whole room erupted into a thunder of singing.

Some of them sang well, and some sang with not much tune or time; and with no accompaniment to keep them together, the singing was ragged and grew gradually slower. But it was deeply enthusiastic and the enjoyment of the singers was intense. Aggie enjoyed herself too, once she had picked up the tune.

After the hymn, there were prayers: people stood up one at a time and prayed about something on their minds. Generally it was sin, though occasionally requests were made for better health for a friend and one gaunt woman prayed for 'a better house, Lord, for we can't hardly live where we're planted now'. When the praying died down a bit there was another hymn, and then there was a break when tea was served from mighty pots and slices of plum cake offered. Aggie did well with the cake. She supposed that after the tea was drunk everybody would go home, but instead of that they all sat down after another hymn and the prayers began again.

By now people were not quite so ready to stand up and speak, and a tall man with whiskers who seemed to be in charge of the proceedings began to invite certain people to pray—generally naming them as Brother Ernie, Brother Charles, Sister Mary and so on (Aggie liked hearing the variety of names). Most of those invited responded by a prayer. After an especially long pause the tall man looked towards the Osgood girls, and said, 'And would one of our young friends lead us in prayer?' Aggie looked at them too. Miriam, the younger, had her eyes screwed shut and her hands gripped together. (That's like she's hiding, Aggie thought.) The elder, Hester, had gone fiercely red and there was water in her eyes.

Something had to be done, and Aggie plunged into the urgent need. She stood up, holding to the chair in front, and launched into her first public prayer.

'O Lord,' she said (that seemed to be the right way to begin). 'I thank you hearty for bringing me to a good place and good people.'

There was a rustle of approval and Aggie was encouraged by her suitable beginning. 'I hope you'll have a care of me because I'm a stranger within the gates,' she went on—remembering a useful phrase she had heard earlier. 'And I pray you'll lead me in a good path and help me to find a place, because I'm on my own in the world, Lord, and I got to make my way and make it honest. And please raise up my dear old granny and give her better legs.' Aggie's thoughts ran dry at this point so she said a loud 'Amen' and sat down.

'Oh thank you!' whispered Hester fervently and seized Aggie's hand, overcome with relief. The two girls sat holding hands until the meeting came to an end.

Several people spoke kindly to Aggie, or at least said goodnight, as the assembly set off for home. The Osgood family clambered into a trap with a married couple whom Aggie identified as Brother Joseph and Sister Ruth.

'I said a prayer, Gran!' announced Aggie, bursting into Granny Flack's house. 'Am I old enough to be Sister Aggie? How old would I have to be?'

'Growed up,' said Gran. 'Sit down, child, do, and quiet yerself down. Chapel's a serious matter.'

'Yes, Gran,' said Aggie, but she hummed a hymn tune as she went to fill the kettle.

EIGHT

The next day needed all Aggie's new confidence: for she was sent for by Mrs Lamb, of Lamb Place, to be interviewed for the post of kitchenmaid. A girl of about eleven, from Miss Marriott's school, delivered a message on her way home at dinnertime. 'If you're Agnes Flack,' she said when Aggie answered Gran's door, 'you're to go to Lamb Place at three o'clock this afternoon.'

'Oh, Gran, I can't!' moaned Aggie when the girl had gone.

'Yes, you can, girl,' said Gran. 'What's to stop you?'

'Just being me,' said Aggie. 'Being stupid and clumsy and all that.'

'Get yer dinner ate,' was all that Gran replied.

So Aggie marched to Lamb Place—near the market, so easy to find—to an encouraging rhyme:

> 'Things ain't so black
> For Aggie Flack—
> Things look good
> Like a Christmas pud.'

But 'Cor blast!' was all she could say at the sight of the house, with its three floors of tall elegant windows set five abreast. At least she did not have to go to the front door, but to the kitchen door and servants' entrance, which was down a small flight of steps with railings round it.

The door was answered, when she knocked, by a skinny boy of about fifteen.

'Agnes Flack, come about a place,' Aggie said, not much above a whisper.

'Oh, really?' said the boy. 'That's odd. I thought you was the Queen of Sheba.'

'Eric!' came a sharp woman's voice from a room close by. 'Show the girl in, and stop fooling.'

'Mrs Ingamells,' muttered Eric, raising his eyebrows. 'In a mood. Watch yer back.'

He pointed to a door opening off the small hall in which they stood. 'Housekeeper's sitting-room,' he said. 'In there.'

Nerving herself, Aggie went in.

Mrs Ingamells, a large stately woman, sat in a high-backed wooden chair. She had an account book open on a small table.

Aggie dropped a half-curtsy. 'Aggie Flack, ma'am,' she said. 'Agnes, I mean.'

'You don't call me ma'am, you call me Mrs Ingamells,' said the housekeeper. 'I understand that Miss Marriott recommends you, though you are not a Marksey girl.'

'I come from Little Needham,' said Aggie. 'There's no work there for a girl. Me gran lives here.'

'Would I know your grandmother? Was she in good service?' asked Mrs Ingamells.

'Not her!' said Aggie. 'She were a cook in a pie shop. She says the customers were tough, but the pies weren't.'

Mrs Ingamells almost smiled. 'And your father and grandfather?' she asked.

'Me father works on the land,' said Aggie. 'I'm not sure about Grandad: he died long since. He had a stall on the market; I think that were china and stuff.'

Mrs Ingamell's questions went on, while Aggie shifted from foot to foot and was half-aware of a chatter of girls' voices and a clatter of crockery from the kitchen nearby.

'I feel disposed to take you, Agnes,' said Mrs Ingamells at last. 'On a month's trial, of course. But mine isn't the last word. I shall take you up to see Mrs Lamb—the mistress.'

'Up' was one flight of wooden stairs with a strip of matting down the middle, then a thick-carpeted staircase to a first-floor sitting-room. Aggie could hardly take it all in—it was a blur of polished wood, heavy dark curtains, shiny ornaments on tables, brownish landscapes in gilt frames. (It must take an army of girls to clean it all, she thought.)

Mrs Lamb sat by a window. She wore black satin, a pair of pince-nez low on her nose; behind them her eyes were blue as thrush-eggs. There was a ferny plant in a round brass pot on a stand beside her and she sat staring at this, her hands in her lap.

'This is the girl Miss Marriott recommends as a kitchenmaid, ma'am,' said Mrs Ingamells. 'Agnes Flack. If I might suggest, ma'am, a month's trial.'

'Are you used to hard work?' demanded Mrs Lamb.

More than you are, I'll lay, thought Aggie. Aloud she said, 'Yes, ma'am. I've helped me mother at home, and me father on the land at whiles.'

Mrs Lamb's questions covered much the same ground as Mrs Ingamells' had done, but ended, 'Are you church or chapel?'

Aggie had to think. Mam was church, Gran was chapel. As she hesitated her eyes rested on the big brass pot; her sight clouded and she swayed as she stood.

Mrs Ingamells saw Aggie's unfixed look and her unsteadiness and put out a hand to support her. Mrs Lamb only said, 'Well? You must be one or the other.'

'Be careful not to fall, Mrs Lamb,' said Aggie in a gasp. 'And watch out for glass. I saw you fallen, and with your arm all cut, and broken glass, and blood. Blood.'

Mrs Lamb's small pale face had grown dark red, and her pince-nez slid further down her nose; she snatched at them and held them, staring at Aggie.

'This is the utmost impertinence,' she said. 'You to warn me! And what do you mean, you saw me?'

'I see things, and they happen,' said Aggie. 'That's all. I don't want it. That just comes.'

'It's unnatural! Uncanny! Of course, you come from the Fens—a backward area,' said Mrs Lamb, who was recovering her poise. 'A region of stunted minds. I'm told witchcraft is still practised there. I know nothing of such things, nor do I wish to. I will certainly not have anyone tainted by the occult in this house. She is not to be engaged, Mrs Ingamells. Send her away.'

'Very good, ma'am,' said Mrs Ingamells, and motioned to Aggie to follow her out.

'Sit down, Agnes,' she said when they got back to her sitting-room. 'Sit still. I'll get you a glass of water.'

Aggie was glad enough to sit and look at the flicker of Mrs Ingamells's coal fire in its narrow grate. She sipped the water thankfully.

'Do you think you can walk back to your grandmother's?' asked Mrs Ingamells, returning after going to scold the girls in the kitchen for their noise.

'I ain't ill, Mrs Ingamells,' said Aggie. 'I feel a bit sickish when I get seeings, but that goes off after a bit.'

'I think what happened to you was a small fit,' said Mrs Ingamells. 'We had a maid here once who took fits, worse than you do; she would fall, and sometimes hurt herself. Talk about seeings and witchcraft is all nonsense. You should see a doctor.'

'Can't afford no doctor,' said Aggie. 'What I want is a place. It's just bad luck I should have a seeing then and scupper me chances with Mrs Lamb.'

'If you're prone to fits, it would have happened sooner or later,' said Mrs Ingamells. 'Don't despair. But get medical advice. Shall I send Eric to walk back with you?'

Aggie certainly didn't fancy Eric's mocking company.

She walked alone. She kept up a dignified pace until she knew she was out of sight of the house; then she ran with all the speed she could to her grandmother's and burst into a torrent of tears on the threshold.

What Aggie wanted then most of all was her mother: Mam to comfort her, Mam to brace her with crisp common sense, Mam to advise on what the next step should be. What she got was Gran in a savage temper—reminding her of Dad, even of Dad when he'd been boozing.

'What's gone wrong, then?' asked Gran sharply as Aggie stumbled into the room. 'Ain't you got the place?'

'No, I ain't,' sobbed Aggie. 'I saw something, Gran, and I told Mrs Lamb, to warn her. She took on awful. And Mrs Ingamells said I had fits.'

'Cor blast! You mucked it up proper,' stormed Gran. 'Couldn't you keep your big mouth shut? I'd pinned all me hopes on Lamb Place for you; you'd have been made. And now what's to become of you? I can't keep you here. The money I get from the chapel people hardly keeps one, and a great girl eating her head off would make short work of me shilling or two.'

'I can't help me seeings, Gran,' said Aggie, swallowing her tears. 'And if I'm spooky, you shouldn't be the one blames me for it. I get that off you.'

'That you never do!' exclaimed Gran, with a snort. 'If you're spooky, ask your mam where you get that from. You're no kin to me.'

'What do you mean?' asked Aggie, shock stopping her sobs. 'Me dad's your son.'

'True enough he's my son, but he ain't your dad,' said Gran. 'Ain't your mam told you? Your real father, he were a travelling-man with a fair; he came to Wisbech when your mam worked there. He sweet-talked her proper and said they'd be married and she were to go away with him when the fair left town. "Come at six in the morning," he said. When she went, there weren't nothing—that fair went off at five.'

'What did he do in the fair?' asked Aggie.

'Ran a shooting gallery,' said Gran. 'The way your mam tells it, he were a handsome man. She loved him, too. You was born out of love, Aggie Flack.'

'So how come she married Dad?' said Aggie.

'Her master sacked her, when she couldn't hide that there was a baby on the way,' said Gran. 'And your dad offered for her and said he'd take you as his own. Whatever bad can be said about him—and there's plenty—he done a kind thing when he done that.'

'Did he love her, then?' asked Aggie, taking in a new possibility. She had never seen any signs of love between Mam and Dad.

'Ah,' said Gran. 'He always fancied her. He lived in Wisbech too, in them days, and he asked her several times. She always thought she could do better for herself, and if it hadn't been for you happening along, she probably could. But there she were, damaged goods, like they say; and he took her on when others she may have liked better would only look the other way.'

'There's good in it for me,' said Aggie, digesting this new light on her mother and her presumed father. 'I ain't his, and that makes it not so bad for me that he turned me out. And there's bad in it: it were because of me Mam had to marry him.'

'He weren't so bad at first,' Gran said. 'They may have been happy for a year or two. You was a pretty little chick of a baby and they had some good days.'

'What am I going to do now, Gran?' said Aggie, coming back down to earth.

'I'm fair put about to know,' said Gran, her bad temper returning. 'What you said to Mrs Lamb, that'll get talked about. Your life's a wreck now. And I can't keep you, girl, so don't think it.'

33

'I got a bit of money,' Aggie offered. 'That'll pay for meals for a little while. But I must get a place—I must. I'll go back to Miss Marriott, after school. Perhaps she can help me again.'

'Ah, perhaps,' said Gran; but she didn't sound very hopeful.

'Damaged goods,' said Aggie to herself as she washed her face in Gran's little scullery before going across to the school. 'Damaged goods. That's what Gran said Mam was, and so am I. Her with a baby coming, and me with like a label hung round me neck saying WITCH. And I couldn't even charm the pimples off Bob Fitch's face—not if I wanted to.'

NINE

Miss Marriott broke into a smile when she opened the schoolhouse door and saw Aggie. 'Agnes!' she exclaimed with pleasure; but then, noticing that Aggie's eyelids were swollen from crying, 'I think you have something to tell me. Come in, lassie; we'll have tea and toast, if you'd like that, and we can talk.'

Aggie's sad story was soon told, and Miss Marriott sighed and shook her head over it. 'It's a shame,' she said. 'But what's done is done, and at least you know you did nothing wrong. Unless it was to say too much.'

'I don't think I could have stopped meself,' said Aggie.

'Maybe not,' said Miss Marriott. 'Let's not think about that. Things need to be done. When we've finished tea I'll take a quick walk and ask a few friends if they know of work to be had.'

'Chapel people?' Aggie asked hopefully. She sensed that she was more likely to meet kindness and acceptance among the chapel people, even though they did almost speak a foreign language. 'But chapel people may have heard why I didn't get the place at Mrs Lamb's. If they think I'm anything to do with magic, they'll be against me.'

'They may not believe what they hear. It's not a very likely story,' said Miss Marriott.

'Well, I suppose,' said Aggie, but she felt her optimism about what the chapel could do for her diminish, and her mind's eye saw smiling faces turn to frowning ones.

'Do you want to wait for me here till I get back?' Miss Marriott asked, as she put on a long cloak and a neat black hat.

'I'll stay,' said Aggie. She welcomed a chance to think in quiet about the happenings of the day.

After Miss Marriott had gone out she sat for some time brooding and staring into the fire. Then, as the early dark had come, she went to the window to draw Miss Marriott's curtains. She looked briefly at her own reflection, as she stood holding the oil-lamp in her hand; and suddenly the focus of her eyes changed, the image blurred, and she was looking at a scene in bright daylight. She herself with a tall man beside her was standing at the top of a hill, looking down at a dark, tangled wood below them. She did not recognize the place, but the man beside her was Brother Joseph from the chapel. In spite of the apparent cheerfulness of the scene she was filled with an appalled and appalling sense of dread.

The oil-lamp rocked and dipped in her hand; she jerked herself back into reality just in time to prevent it from falling. Like an automaton she drew the curtains, put the lamp on the table and went back to the fire; but the horror of her vision would not leave her and she sat shivering and tearful, fighting off nausea.

'Not twice in one day!' she groaned to herself. 'That's not fair. That's never been twice in one day.'

Miss Marriott, returning, was shocked to find her in such a state.

'Has anything happened to upset you?' she asked Aggie anxiously.

Aggie tried to put her seeing into words, but could not. Anyway it was nonsense—not like the drowned baby, or Mrs Lamb's fall, which were possibilities anyone could understand. 'It's me thoughts,' was all she could say by way of explanation.

'It's no wonder,' said Miss Marriott. 'Things have been happening to you too fast. I'll make us some soup, Aggie; you sit there and keep warm.'

'Did you find anything for me?' said **Aggie** as they drank their soup by the fire.

'It's hopeful,' said Miss Marriott. 'No promises, but it's hopeful. Baxter's the drapers are doing very well and may be taking on extra staff; and there may be a place going on a farm.'

'Baxter's won't take me,' said Aggie. 'They'd be afraid of offending Mrs Lamb.'

'Well, maybe,' said Miss Marriott. 'I don't know whether the place on the farm will do for you, Aggie—if there really is a place on a farm. Brother Ernie is going to find out. The farm that he thinks may be looking for a girl sounds like a rough place; you'd be maid-of-all-work in the house and might even be expected to help out on the farm at times.'

'I could do it,' said Aggie instantly. 'I'm no china image, Miss Marriott. I'm rough meself and I come from the rough Fens and I couldn't be ladylike if I tried. I'm strong, too.'

'I'm sure you are,' said Miss Marriott soothingly. 'But you're so young, Aggie; too young to be all alone in a place like that.'

'Ain't there no children?' asked Aggie.

'Not that I heard of,' said Miss Marriott. 'But let's not think about it. Can you play cards?'

'Ain't it wicked?' asked Aggie, who thought chapel people frowned on all games.

'Patience isn't wicked,' said Miss Marriott. 'Patience is a virtue—haven't you heard?'

'Yes, I heard,' said Aggie. 'Patience is a virtue,

> Possess it if you can,
> Seldom in a woman,
> Never in a man.

I do wish I'd written that.'

Miss Marriott exploded into laughter and two

cheerful people sat down at the table and played cards until Miss Marriott sent Aggie back to Gran's and the little bed up Gran's narrow stairs. Against all her expectations, Aggie slept without nightmares—no Mrs Lamb with her arm pouring blood, no Brother Joseph standing above the dark wood.

TEN

Virtuous or not, Aggie was deeply impatient to get something settled for the next stage of her life. She must get a place and keep it and leave with training and a character and a bit in her pocket for Mam—to help out with Sam's and Melia's clothes and perhaps to buy Mam a treat for herself.

She spent an energetic day shopping for Gran (spending a little of the money Mam had given her) and giving the little almshouse a spring-clean. When the light began to fail she and Gran sat down to a pot of tea.

Their tea-drinking was interrupted by the large, broad-faced, jovial man whom Aggie knew as Brother Ernie. He accepted a cup of tea and sat down at the fireside.

'Well, this is cosy,' he said. 'We must be thankful to the Lord for all his mercies. And I've got good news for Aggie, though perhaps not the best I could have brought you. Baxter's ain't taking on new staff. But the Gutteridges out at North Lode Farm, they're wanting a maid and they're wanting her at once. Now, do you think it's the place for you, young Aggie? It'll be hard work and heavy work, and I can't speak for the Gutteridges as masters—they ain't chapel folk. They may be good enough people, all the same,' he added generously.

'I'll try it, and thank you,' said Aggie without hesitation.

'Think what you're taking on, Aggie,' Brother Ernie urged. 'It's a long way out of town, and you'll have no company but the two of them.'

'I'll try it,' repeated Aggie. 'If I can get there. Can I walk it in a day?'

'Brother George goes out that way for milk,' said Ernie. 'He goes round them country farms, real early, picking up the milk. He'll take you. Be at Hobbs's dairy, right on six. I'll be on me way, then, ladies. I've left the wife with me stall in the market and if I ain't there she'll sell things off too cheap—she likes to get stuff cleared, my Flo does. The Lord loveth a cheerful giver, but trade's trade,' he added, leaving Aggie doubting the logic of his views.

'I ought to thank you proper, but I don't know your name, except Ernie,' said Aggie, holding out her hand.

The big man shook her hand and then patted her shoulder. 'Ernest Shutter, and may the Lord bless you,' he said. 'Be of good courage, Matthew four, ten. Hobbs's dairy, sharp at six. Peace be on this house.'

Sharp on six it was: Aggie was there in the half-dark of the grey morning. George was already up on his milk-cart with its load of empty churns, and gave a hand to Aggie to pull her up beside him.

'Thank you, Mr Hobbs,' she said. 'I can pay me fare.'

'Ah, you can do that,' said George and grinned. 'Now hold tight, Miss Aggie; we're off and Old Blossom's going to trot.'

Aggie hoped Old Blossom (who didn't look old at all, but a smart brown cob) knew the way in the near dark as well as Old Violet had done. She tucked her chilly fingers into her coat-sleeves and wondered if George's route took him near Little Needham. As the light grew, and George stopped at various farm gates to pick up full churns and pails, she realized that he was going the other side of Marksey. They went through several villages she had never seen, and in one stopped at a red-brick farmhouse with white painted window-frames, a garden in front and a farmyard at the side.

'Willetts' farm—Brother Joseph's,' said George as he got down from the cart, giving Aggie the reins.

'So he's Joseph Willett,' said Aggie. 'He don't live near hills and woods, then, Mr Hobbs?'

'See for yerself,' said George, chinking the lid of the churn at the farmhouse gate. 'The Osgoods live round the corner, but this here's Joseph's.'

The journey ended with a long ride along a poor, narrow road, and they drew up at an isolated farm. The house was of dirty yellowish brick and there were ramshackle outhouses around it. Up to it led a long, rutted, deeply muddy track.

'North Lode Farm,' said George. 'I can't take me cart up that track, Aggie, so I'll have to set you down here. And I'll have me fare first.'

Aggie felt for her purse.

'Not money, you goose,' said George. 'I'll have a kiss, Aggie.'

'George Hobbs! And I thought you was chapel,' said Aggie.

'Chapel is as chapel does,' said George, roaring with laughter, and gave her a smacking kiss on the cheek. 'And remember,' he shouted down to her as he drove away, after picking up the North Lode milk, 'if you can't stand it, be here same time tomorrow. And I'll take you back.'

It can't be that bad, thought Aggie as she made her way up the track. I'll make a go of it. To avoid the deepest mud and ruts she walked at the edge of the track, where sparse grass struggled through the dirt, and defiantly lifted the blackened knocker and thumped the front door. Someone had been up and done the milking, she reasoned; somebody must be about. The only answer she got was a woman's head, hair sticking out at all angles, poked out of an upstairs window.

'Go round the back!' shouted the owner of the head. 'We ain't up yet.'

'I'm the new girl,' Aggie called up.

'What did you think I thought you was—the Angel Gabriel?' answered the tufty head. 'I said, round the back!'

'Goodnight!' muttered Aggie expressing her disgust. She heaved up the carpet-bag and made for the back of the house. Here, a one-eyed collie on a strong chain barked its head off at her. Reckoning that there was no point in trying the back door—which was being guarded by the dog—she looked for shelter from the raw, damp morning air, and found her way into the cowshed where the cows breathed out a sweet warmth.

These old girls ain't been milked today, thought Aggie. That must've been yesterday's milk George Hobbs got given; hope he knew. Well, what needs doing needs doing.

Dad had taught her to milk, long ago, when he had given a hand with Bowleses' cows. Aggie fetched a pail and a stool, snuggled up to the first cow, and sang to it as she milked. It seemed a happy and a peaceful way to begin a new job.

When the back door of the farm finally opened and a grimy, unshaven man appeared at it, yawning and stretching, Aggie marched towards him across the corner of the yard, her bag in one hand and a full pail in the other.

'Aggie Flack,' she said. 'Come to work for you. I got your milking done.'

Eleven

Aggie thought she might get at least a nod of acknowledgement. Mr Gutteridge, however, merely hawked his throat clear and spat in the farmyard mud.

Aggie looked at him, and he looked at her. She saw a tall, lanky man with hollowed cheeks and a yellowish, waxy skin. She thought he looked ill and rather as though he didn't get enough to eat; his clothes too were worn and casually mended with patches of different material.

When at last he spoke all he said was, 'You was hired to help me missus, not to milk cows. Get in the house. Put the milk in the kitchen.'

'Yes, Mr Gutteridge,' said Aggie. Every instinct rebelled against calling him sir.

He had omitted to tell her where the kitchen was, but Aggie heard a pan clatter in a room ahead of her and went that way, through the scullery. She found there the owner of the tufty head, a skinny woman with a brown overall wrapped around her angles. She was stirring an iron pot on the hob.

'Put that milk down, and come and stir this porridge,' snapped Mrs Gutteridge. 'Don't you do the milking again—that's his job, the lazy coot. Milk goes on the slab over there. Now get your coat off, gal, and come and get stirring. Work was what you come here for—or ain't you got the message?'

'I got it,' said Aggie. She peeled off her coat and advanced on the pot.

'You ain't dressed for work, are you?' asked Mrs Gutteridge with heavy sarcasm, looking at Aggie's tidy black dress. 'Cor blast, gal, where you been working? At the Bishop's Palace?'

'I could wear me school clothes, Mrs Gutteridge, but I got no apron,' said Aggie.

'It's to be hoped your ideas of work don't match your fancy clothes,' said Mrs Gutteridge with a sniff. 'You can change after breakfast. Take this.'

She pushed a wooden spoon into Aggie's hand and herself went to the table to cut doorsteps of bread off a white loaf. The table was littered with old newspapers, dirty crockery, Mr Gutteridge's pipes and tobacco, and even—Aggie saw with sardonic amusement—a dead mouse in a mouse-trap.

Breakfast was eaten off this cluttered table (after Aggie had unbidden removed the mouse); Aggie was told to take her seat with the Gutteridges. If the house had not been such a pigsty she might have felt it was promotion to eat with the master and mistress. However, they got thick slices of bacon and she didn't: except that after Mr Gutteridge had picked at his and only half finished it Mrs Gutteridge ordered him, 'If you ain't going to eat that, Bernard, give it to the gal.' Aggie made no fuss about eating other people's leavings; she had a feeling she would have to fend for herself as best she could in this house.

Her own room was a tiny attic, with a broken window-pane through which cold Fenland air streamed in, and a damp patch in the ceiling which must mean a slipped or broken roof-tile up above. There was no cupboard, but a rail in one corner where Aggie could hang a few things. There was no washstand; Aggie presumed she had to wash at the pump downstairs. She sniffed to express her feelings and changed into her old school skirt and a dark jumper.

'That's better,' said Mrs Gutteridge when Aggie went downstairs again. 'I got no spare apron for you, gal; you'll have to use sacks.'

Mrs Gutteridge found her two sacks and some large

safety-pins, and Aggie pinned one sack to the shoulders of her jumper and wrapped another one around her skirt. They smelt of jute, a strong throat-catching smell, and faintly of meal. Dressed like this, Aggie got down on her knees and began the job of scrubbing the brick floors with cold water.

> 'Aggie Flack
> Wrapped in a sack—
> Oh, Mrs Ingamells, take me back!'

she muttered in time with her scrubbing.

There was never anything but cold water at North Lode—except when Mrs Gutteridge was making one of her frequent pots of tea. Aggie on that first day asked Mrs Gutteridge if she could boil up a kettle of water to help her tackle the dinnertime pots and pans; Mrs Gutteridge said it was unnecessary and the things would easily enough scrape clean, with the help of washing-soda. Grimly Aggie scraped, her usual tool being a dinner-knife with a broken handle. After a few days of North Lode, her hands were rough and red and disfigured with chaps and painful chilblains, which cracked open and wept. She had never worked so hard or been so cold; or, she sometimes thought, eaten so little, even when times were hard at home. If she had not had the scraps Mr Gutteridge left she would have gone even hungrier.

As the days went by she reached what she felt was a fair estimate of the characters of her employers. Mrs Gutteridge was lazy, heartless, and mean, and was generally uttering a complaint about the idleness of her husband or Aggie, while she herself did as little as she could. Mr Gutteridge was all right in his way, but disorganized; and, she became more and more convinced, ill. He had dark rings under his eyes, and blueish fingernails. He shivered often and would get so

45

close to the kitchen fire to warm himself that you could smell his trousers singeing.

The pattern of life at North Lode did not include any time off for Aggie; and she wondered sadly where she would go if she did get any. If her sense of the distance travelled in George Hobbs's cart was at all accurate, it was too far to walk to Gran's and back in half a day. Perhaps when the summer came she might get some time to explore the Lode and walk in the meadows around.

One Sunday morning she was scraping the porridge pot with a knife wrapped in a dishcloth, all her chaps and chilblains hurting and no hope in her. She was stuck out here in these black Fens with—as Brother Ernie had warned her—no company but the Gutteridges and no prospect of getting any.

She was in the scullery which opened off the kitchen, and whose main features were a cracked window and a huge sink; the Gutteridges were in the kitchen, not talking much to each other, and the only sounds in the house were the ticking of the kitchen clock and Aggie's determined scraping. The knock at the front door sounded through the open doors of sitting-room and hallway.

'Whoever can that be, Bernard!' exclaimed Mrs Gutteridge.

'How should I know?' murmured Mr Gutteridge, who seemed half-asleep.

'Nobody comes to the front,' said Mrs Gutteridge.

'Shall I go?' called Aggie.

'All right, then, but get the sacks off you,' Mrs Gutteridge called back.

Aggie upended the porridge pot, now as clean as it would ever be; tore off her sacks, scattering safety-pins; and almost ran to the front door, tormented with curiosity.

46

Outside, smart in his Sunday best, stood Mr Osgood.

'I've come to fetch you to chapel, Aggie,' he said, and he smiled. Aggie thought he looked like an angel. In the distance at the end of the farm track she could see his neat trap, with Mrs Osgood holding the reins; she saw Hester and Miriam wave.

'Oh, Mr Osgood, I'd love to come,' she said. 'I'll have to ask.'

TWELVE

'Time off to go to chapel? I never heard the like!' exclaimed Mrs Gutteridge when Aggie asked.

'Let her go, Ida. It'll do no harm,' said Mr Gutteridge. 'She works hard enough. Give her her outing.'

Aggie couldn't see Mr Gutteridge winning this argument. 'Will you come to the front and speak to Mr Osgood?' she urged Mrs Gutteridge. 'He'll want to know why I can't go, when he's come special to fetch me.'

Mrs Gutteridge grumpily went. Mr Osgood took his bowler hat off to her and politely repeated his request.

'I see no call for chapelgoing,' said Mrs Gutteridge, her arms folded across her chest and her eyes flashing aggression.

Mr Osgood took the measure of her. 'It's the law, ma'am,' he said with civil firmness. 'England's a Christian country: we've got freedom of worship. If she wants to go to chapel, she's got the right.'

Mrs Gutteridge snorted, but she was on uncertain ground, having no knowledge of the law herself. 'Get your coat, then, Aggie,' she said. 'How will you get back?'

'I'll bring her, ma'am,' said Mr Osgood. 'Late afternoon. There's an afternoon service, too, of course.'

'Seems some people never work,' said Mrs Gutteridge as Aggie ran for her coat.

'Six days shalt thou labour,' said Mr Osgood. 'We all do that. But remember the Sabbath Day, to keep it holy.'

Mrs Gutteridge said something that sounded like 'Drat the Sabbath!' and stumped back to her kitchen.

'I thought I'd never get out of that place, Mr Osgood, not for chapel or anything,' said Aggie as they picked their way along the farm track. 'This is a marvel—your poor boots, though!' she added as they came off the track on to the road. The boots of both of them were thickly muddy in spite of all the hopping they had done.

'Hand me down the scraper, Lizzie, my dear,' said Mr Osgood to his wife. He scraped Aggie's boots more or less clean, and Aggie scraped his; and the trap headed for town with the three girls chattering in the back. Now that Hester and Miriam knew Aggie they had plenty to say; and they listened enthralled to Aggie's account of life with the Gutteridges.

Aggie had not thought, on her first visit to the chapel, that going there could ever be a pleasure and a treat; but it was a treat for her today. She looked around when the Osgood party had sat down, pleased to see faces she recognized; and she exchanged smiles with Miss Marriott. Her only grief was that when her hands got warm in the heat of the stoves, her chilblains tormented her worse with pain and itching than they had done in the damp cold of North Lode.

She had not previously stayed for an afternoon service, but as the Osgoods plainly meant to she had no choice today. The morning service finished about half-past twelve, and then kettles were put on to make tea, and sandwiches and cake were brought out. Aggie had brought no food, but Mrs Osgood said they had enough for her and other people came up to offer some of theirs. Miss Marriott contributed cake and George Hobbs a rather shrunken apple. But best of all, sweet-faced Mrs Willett carried a little meat-pie over to her and put it into her hand. 'If you can't eat it now, take it back with you,' she said. 'I daresay you could do with it.'

Aggie smiled her gratitude.

'John the Baptist is said to have lived on locusts,' Mr Willett called over to her; 'but even he couldn't live on black beetles, I imagine.'

Cor blast, thought Aggie, has he been to North Lode?

The afternoon service did not begin until two, so all the people who were not local went for walks in the town after their picnic lunch. Aggie paid a quick visit to Gran, waking her out of her afternoon sleep.

'What's it like, then, your place?' asked Gran, poking her little fire.

'Cold and black and mean, Gran, that's what it's like,' said Aggie with a sigh.

'Ah,' said Gran, holding her thin hands to the fire. 'There's news from Lamb Place since you went. Old Mrs Lamb, she fell—tripped over the edge of a mat, the story goes, and came down crash. Cut her arm on a wineglass and knocked herself silly.'

'She'll believe me now,' said Aggie.

'Yes, and blame you for witchcraft,' said Gran. 'You daft besom!'

'We been over all that once, Gran,' said Aggie wearily. 'I'm going back to the chapel. If you see anyone from home get a message to Mam that I'm all right at the Gutteridges. I'll make a go of it.'

'When do I ever see folk from Little Needham?' was all Gran said; but she did add, as Aggie turned to say goodbye at the door, 'Dip those chilblains into your chamber-pot, nights. Piss is the best there is for chilblains.'

Aggie nursed her tingling hands through the afternoon service, and drowsed the sermon away; but the drive home through chilly air waked her, and she climbed down alertly when the trap reached North Lode Farm.

'Now remember,' said Mr Osgood, 'I'll come for you next Sunday.'

'I'll watch for you, and come down the track on me own,' said Aggie. 'That'll be only one pair of boots to scrape.'

'And Saturday week, I'll come in the afternoon and take you to the young people's meeting,' he said. 'Afternoon, with tea, at the Willetts' farm. Tell her it's the law!'

Aggie went up the track to the dark farmhouse at a scrambling run, full of the cheerfulness of friendly company.

The Gutteridges' kitchen was empty, the fire almost out; Aggie wondered for a moment if they had gone visiting—but where, in that empty landscape?

As she stood considering, Mr Gutteridge came shuffling in from the yard, a pail of milk carried with both hands in front of him. He set it down, laid a finger on his lips as Aggie was about to speak to him, and whispered, 'Speak low—she's upstairs having a sleep, but she sleeps like a fly—anything'll wake her. Now, Aggie Flack, now's our chance. Can you help me?'

THIRTEEN

Aggie stood dumbstruck, her mind in a whirl. Surely Mr Gutteridge was not a dirty old man; but what else could he mean?

'She keeps me short,' said Mr Gutteridge, puffing with the urgency of what he had to say. 'I only get me baccy money. She won't give me no more. I can't get the stuff. You can see I'm bad, gal, with the shakes. You're a Flack: they're knowers, the Flacks. I thought you might know something; you could help.'

Comprehension dawned on Aggie, and with it, despair. Even in this godforsaken hole she was known, or mis-known; she was considered a witch.

'You mean, the Fen Ague?' she said to Mr Gutteridge.

'That's what I said—the shakes,' said Mr Gutteridge. 'I'm bad with it, Aggie; fair awful.'

Aggie understood now what his pallor and his lassitude and his wretched shivering must mean: malaria was common in the Fens, where mosquitoes bred richly in slow and stagnant water. Many people died of this debilitating misery. What they took for it was laudanum, or opium—'the stuff'.

'Can't you grow it?' she asked him. 'They grow it in our village; the poppies look pretty when they're out.'

'Oh, I tried,' said Mr Gutteridge, 'I tried. But last summer, we got not near enough sun and the poppies was little spindly things without much juice in them. If I'd got money I could buy the stuff, but like I said, she don't let me have enough.'

Aggie felt sorry for his obvious illness and almost regretted disappointing him.

'I can't help, no, Mr Gutteridge,' she said. 'I ain't a

knower: I never got that off the Flacks.' She would have loved to add that she was no kin to the Flacks, but her mother's secret must be kept.

Tears gathered in Mr Gutteridge's eyes. 'You don't know herbs and cures, then?' he persisted.

'Not for the ague,' said Aggie. 'I only know what everybody knows.'

Mr Gutteridge wiped his eyes with the back of his hand. 'If anything comes to you—like it might be a charm, Aggie—you come to me quiet-like and say,' he said. 'I'm fair desperate.'

'Do you want a pot of tea made?' offered Aggie; but Mr Gutteridge shook his head.

'You'd best get on with some work,' he said. 'Or she'll be after you when she comes down.'

'I best had,' agreed Aggie, as she pinned on her sacks and put her chilblains back into cold water to wash the crockery left for her after the Gutteridges' dinner.

If it had not been for the cold water, and the dirt of ages in the house and the scanty food, and Mrs Gutteridge's sour temper, Aggie might almost have come to enjoy life at North Lode Farm. She was not completely trapped: she could at times escape to the world of chapel with sometimes a visit to Gran thrown in. She began to feel that the grim little scullery was her kingdom. She even made forays into Mrs Gutteridge's kitchen and parlour and brought back assorted china to wash. She discovered too that a black and dented teapot was silver; Mrs Gutteridge found some silver polish and a piece of ancient sheet so that Aggie could clean it up. Aggie saved this job for a day when she was not rushed off her feet.

This day came at last when both the Gutteridges went to Marksey. Aggie was left in charge, and sang around the house with her broom. She milked the cows and fed the hens, and took potato peelings to the Gutteridges' solitary pig, and enjoyed feeling useful and efficient. 'Get what pleasure you can from it, girl,' she said to herself. 'You won't get no thanks.'

When all this was done, she tore up the sheeting to make several cloths and sat down with the teapot and got polishing. As she had hoped, the pot polished up to a soft moony shine. She finally buffed it with the cleanest of the cloths and sat looking at it with pride. But as she did, her reflected face dissolved, as it had dissolved in Mam's spoon or Miss Marriott's window, and she was looking again at the bright hillside and the tangle of wood below it. Only this time, she was further down the hill than in her earlier seeing. Her horror came back to her; and even though she returned to a right sense of herself and the teapot and the kitchen, the fear kept her shuddering for the rest of that day.

She did not fully shake off the low spirits this seeing brought until the next Saturday, when Mr Osgood took her as promised to the young people's meeting at Willetts' farm. This was pure joy. George Hobbs had brought several passengers from Marksey; the Osgood girls were there and three children had come on foot from the nearest village, Frog End.

The Willetts' house had a capacious sitting-and-dining room, with a settle and two sofas and a big table surrounded by wheelback chairs. Somehow, twelve young visitors squeezed into this, plus the Willetts themselves and their two small children, twins of about two years old. George Hobbs went off, after delivering his cargo, to visit a Hardingley girl he had taken a fancy to.

It was meant to be a serious meeting, but with so many young people together the serious side was swamped by the fun and jokes; and after what Aggie called a thundering good tea Mr Willett pushed back the table and set up various party games.

Aggie went home with Mr Osgood, full of happiness and hope, with a piece of cake in her pocket 'for tomorrow' as Mrs Willett had said.

Just after Christmas (which had brought no holiday for Aggie) she was amazed one morning to see a postman toiling up the North Lode track. She realized she had taken it for granted that the Gutteridges never got post. The letter was for Mrs Gutteridge, who opened it nervously.

'That looks like our Bertha's hand,' she said to her husband as she did this. 'Yes, danged if it ain't.' And as she read, 'Blast it, Bernard, if she ain't coming here!'

'What for?' demanded Mr Gutteridge.

'Danged if I know,' said Mrs Gutteridge. 'That husband of hers is bringing her over. Tomorrow, that'll be. Save us, Bernard—they'll be wanting dinner!'

They'll be lucky, thought Aggie, immensely entertained.

'Don't you just stand there, Aggie!' scolded Mrs Gutteridge. 'You know what company means. Get to polishing in the parlour—go on! No, do the carpets first. Get them outside and wallop them.'

The rest of the day was a turmoil of cleaning and tidying. Mr Gutteridge sensibly disappeared about his farm work while Aggie endured a conflicting and increasingly shrill cascade of orders from Mrs Gutteridge. The crescendo culminated with a shriek from Mrs Gutteridge, at the end of the afternoon: 'Aggie, you thieving varmint! Where's me silver teapot?'

Fourteen

'Where I put it, I'm sure, Mrs Gutteridge,' Aggie called back. 'In the china cupboard.'

'No it ain't!' yelled Mrs Gutteridge. 'You come here and point to where you put it.'

Aggie went, and saw distinctly on the middle shelf of the cupboard the space where the teapot should have been.

'That's where I put it,' she said. 'Ain't you moved it yourself?'

''Course I ain't,' shrilled Mrs Gutteridge. 'Bernard! Bernard!'—as she heard him clanking in with his milk-pail—'Get yourself in here. This thieving besom's made off with me teapot!'

Mr Gutteridge came in, an oil-lamp in his hand. The glow lit up his expression as he fixed his eyes on Aggie. She read in it a mingling of shame, fear, and entreaty. She knew at once where the teapot had gone: pawned, or sold, to buy the laudanum that eased the shakes.

'I ain't had it, Mrs Gutteridge,' she reiterated. 'Ain't it got pushed to the back of the cupboard? Take a look.'

Mrs Gutteridge snatched the lamp from her husband and clattered and tinkled the contents of the cupboard. 'Ain't no teapot here,' she finally said. 'As you know right well, Aggie Flack. Because you've took it, ain't you?'

'No,' said Aggie stoutly. 'No, I ain't. What would I do with a silver teapot?'

'Sell it, of course,' snapped Mrs Gutteridge. 'Some of your righteous chapel friends, like as not. That smarmy Osgood what knows all about law—he'd give you money for a silver pot.'

'Do I look as if I got money?' said Aggie.

'You'd have more sense than to show it,' said Mrs Gutteridge. 'You can get out of here, this minute, and be thankful I don't get the Law to you. Your Mr Osgood wouldn't be able to help you then.'

Aggie drew in a deep breath to say 'Get the Law, then': but she let it out again. A servant-girl in her first post would not stand up well in court against the determined fury of Mrs Gutteridge—and the silence of her husband. She shot one glance at Mr Gutteridge. He looked at her quickly, a look of beseeching, and cast his eyes down to his boots.

'If you say I got to go, then I'll go,' she said. 'But I never took no teapot, and I'll die saying it. I suppose you'll let me stay till morning, seeing it's dark as the grave outside, and raining.'

'No, I won't,' said Mrs Gutteridge with decision. 'You come in the dark. You can go in the dark.'

'I got nowhere to go,' said Aggie, her bravado swamped by real fear. 'I'd fall into them old drains and I'd drown.'

'The devil looks after his own,' said Mrs Gutteridge. 'You got ten minutes to pack.'

In silence Aggie took a candle and trudged up the narrow stairs to her attic; and in silence she tumbled her few possessions into the old carpet-bag.

When she got downstairs again there was no sign of Mr Gutteridge; Mrs Gutteridge stood with folded arms at the foot of the stairs.

'Don't you owe me nothing?' asked Aggie boldly. 'I've worked a month, and over.'

'Owe you?' shrieked Mrs Gutteridge. 'Owe you! When you've had me best teapot, and me only silver! That was me mam's, that was, and her mam's before her. Get out that door, and stay out; and if I ever see you again, I don't know what I won't do!' She gave

Aggie a push in the small of the back which sent her hurtling out into the dark and the mud of the track.

In the moonless night, Aggie slipped and squelched in the muddy ruts. Once out on the road she managed a little better. She found that if she kept walking with one foot in a dryish rut—not a rut that had a continuous puddle all the way along it—she could keep going in a reasonably straight line. She headed the way George Hobbs had brought her. Somewhere along that route, if she could only get to it, was Hardingley where the Willett and Osgood families lived. If she could find somebody to direct her to the Osgoods' house, they would surely stretch their kindness to her a little further, and let her stay for the night?

As she stumbled on, her right foot always feeling for the edge of the rut, she prayed for someone to help her, direct her, give her a lift. Or at least for a gleam of moonlight. Or if not that, at least for an end to the rain.

The rain did let up, but Aggie very nearly got wetter than any rain could have made her. She remembered that the side-road to the Gutteridges' farm turned off at a T-junction; she had forgotten that along the side of the road it joined, ran a deep drain. When her feet lost the rut they were following and got tangled up in a criss-crossing muddle of other ruts and bumps, she went straight forward instead of turning. She suddenly found herself on a slippery slope, on her back, her feet shooting from under her—and knew she had met the ditch.

It was not the first time in her life that Aggie had slid towards water. She dug in her heels, dug in the carpet-bag, clutched grass with her empty hand; and managed to stop her headlong descent. Hanging there, she listened: the susurration of water seemed only a foot below.

Inch by inch, using her heels as levers and her free hand to haul on tufts of grass, Aggie worked her way up the bank. There was one awful moment when one of her heels caught in the hem of her coat and she lost purchase and slipped again towards the water: she only saved herself by an energetic use of the other heel.

When at last she got to the top of the bank, she sat, shuddering and crying, and considered.

'Stay where you are, Aggie Flack,' she told herself. 'You can't see that old water, but that old water can see you. Stay put and wait till daylight: all you can do.'

She settled herself at the top of the bank, with her head on her knees and the bag close beside her; and in that unlikely position she fell asleep.

An agony of stiffness woke her; and to her relief and delight she woke into an eerie, stormy moonlight. A wind had got up and was driving ragged violet strips of cloud across the moon; but the moon was bright behind them.

Aggie swung her arms and stamped, then set off towards—she hoped—the Osgoods. Although she was glad to have slept the moonless stretch of the night away, she guessed it was now late and that she had little or no chance of meeting a trap or cart—or even someone she could ask for directions—along the way. Her guess was right. She walked on, more and more weary and footsore, and only once met another human being: a short, stout man rolling along the deserted road, presumably from a public house or a hospitable neighbour's. Aggie judged it was no use asking him for help, and ducked down into the shadow of a twiggy elder bush until he had gone by.

By the time she came to the village between North Lode and Hardingley, she was very tired and very lonely. A few upstairs windows here showed lamplight, but most of the windows were unlit. Worse, the moon's light was only fitful now, as clouds grew heavier and the wind died away.

'Keep it up, moon,' breathed Aggie as she plodded along. 'Wish I'd had me tea before I left North Lode—I do, I do. Wish me feet didn't hurt. Wish I were still little and Dad couldn't throw me out and I were still at home . . .'

She thought of home, and tramped on; and suddenly in a good patch of moonlight she saw buildings ahead— a pigsty, a barn. Hardingley. But nobody was in the streets, all the windows were dark. How could she find the Osgoods? Did she dare knock on a door, wake sleepers, and ask?

'I never could,' muttered Aggie. She stood, when she came to it, outside the Willetts' farm—there was still enough moonlight for her to recognize that—where the chapel children had met, where there had been laughter and lashings of food. The downstairs windows were shuttered and there was no gleam of light.

'I'd have slept in the Gutteridges' cowshed, if I'd had the chance,' said Aggie to herself. 'Willetts' cowshed'll be much the same.'

She pushed the big farm gate a little way open and squeezed through. No dog barked in the farmyard. She trod quietly, trying in the sliding moonlight to avoid deep mud. She passed the back door of the farmhouse; and then, just beyond a large stone trough, saw a half-door. She unlatched the top half of this, creaked it just open, and peered in. Two huge heads swung towards her and she heard the heavy snuffling breath of cart-horses, blowing down inquisitive noses. Where there are stables there are haylofts, but Aggie couldn't see, in the stable's shadows, where the ladder went up; nor did she want to risk the uncertain welcome of strange horses. She pushed the half-door shut and went on to the next outbuilding. She passed a lofty open-sided shed with waggons and a trap inside, and came then to a smaller building, also open along one side, where bales of straw were stacked and a pile of loose straw lay collapsed on the ground. Not so warm as a closed shed, thought Aggie, but the straw was a bonus.

Her soaked boots and damp coat and hat came off. She made a thick layer of straw for her mattress, and tugged more straw over her as she lay, until she was cocooned in a tickling straw eiderdown. She did her best to draw her coat over this to keep the straw in place. Sleep got the better of her before her unaccustomed bedding was properly sorted out, and swallowed her into its release.

FIFTEEN

A voice, and the light of a lantern, startled Aggie awake. The voice said, 'What's this?' in a stern growl and the light slid over Aggie's shut eyes. She struggled awake and sat up, straw clinging to her hair and her jumper. There was only a little daylight, but the lamplight was bright enough for her to recognize Mr Willett. He evidently didn't recognize her; and with all that straw about her, Aggie didn't blame him.

'It's Aggie Flack, Mr Willett,' she said; and immediately sneezed from the effect of the dust in the straw.

'And what are you doing in my straw-stack, Aggie Flack?' asked Mr Willett. This time he sounded a bit less severe—almost as if he could see the funny side of it.

'Trespassing, I expect,' said Aggie. 'I'm sorry, Mr Willett; I never meant to. I got throwed out of Gutteridges', and it were dark, and rain falling, and I as near as dammit fell in the drain, so I had to stay where I were till the moon came up. Then I walked here, and I meant to find Osgoods and ask them if I could sleep on their floor or somewhere. But I don't know where they live and there were nobody to ask, and I knew you lived here and I came looking for the cowshed.'

'I see,' said Mr Willett. 'And why did Gutteridges throw you out?'

'Mrs Gutteridge said I'd had her silver teapot,' said Aggie. 'But I never did.'

Mr Willett eyed her quizzically and Aggie burst into tears. 'You don't believe me!' she sobbed. 'Nobody believes me. But I don't tell lies and I want to keep a place and better meself and be Sister Aggie.'

'Here, stand up,' said Mr Willett. He put down his lantern and used both hands to pull her to her feet. 'My wife had better sort this out. Get your feet into your boots, Aggie, and go into the house—see the light through the cracks around the door? The kitchen's on your left. Tell my wife all about it and get her to give you breakfast. I'll be in when I've done the cows.'

'Breakfast' was as a magic word to Aggie. She didn't bother to button up her boots or put on her coat and hat, and appeared in Mrs Willett's kitchen as a vision of misery and disrepair—a lot of straw still hung on her, and tear-tracks on her face.

Mrs Willett was standing at her kitchen range, heating milk in a saucepan.

'Well, Aggie,' she said, 'come to breakfast? That's good, I could just use another pair of hands. Hang your coat over the chair-back and come and watch this milk, while I get the children up; they're wide awake and Albie's fallen out of his cot once. Take the milk off just before it boils.'

Mrs Willett lit herself a candle and hurried out, while Aggie watched the milk and warmed herself in the heat of the stove. The kitchen was bright with lamplight, clean and cheerful, with willow pattern plates already set out on a yellow tablecloth. Aggie enjoyed it richly.

While Mrs Willett was still upstairs, Mr Willett came in with his pails of milk and clattered into the room which opened off the kitchen. This farm had a proper dairy, Aggie realized. He got back into the kitchen before his wife did.

'That milk's hot enough,' he said to Aggie. 'Take yourself a candle and spruce yourself up—our wash-place is just past the yard door.'

Aggie found the wash-place, with an earth closet, a

dipper of clean water, and a mirror on the wall. She brushed herself free of straw as best she could, but kept her eyes off the mirror. She did not want to see the bright hillside and the dark wood again.

When she got back to the kitchen she found the Willetts, each with a small child on its knee and in the act of spooning bread and milk into it. The children, Albie and Flora, were not co-operating but competing for the attention of a half-grown cat which was playing with its own tail on an empty chair.

'Tip the cat off, Aggie, and sit down,' said Mr Willett.

'Shall I take one of the children? I'm used to children,' said Aggie.

'Not till you've eaten yourself, child,' said Mr Willett. 'You are our guest.'

Feeling suitably grand, Aggie ate bread with thick honey, and drank tea, while the Willetts talked about pigs and butter and the concerns of the village. When she had finished, she offered again to take a child.

'That would be good,' said Mrs Willett. 'Take Albie, will you; I'll do Joseph a bit of bacon.'

Aggie took the wriggling Albie, noticing as she did so that Ruth Willett's next child would not be long in coming. 'Now then, Albie,' she said, and got a mouthful of bread and milk into him before he had realized what she was up to.

Ruth Willett gave her husband his bacon, poured them all fresh tea and said, 'Let's have your story, then, Aggie. I can see there is a story.'

The story was told over the heads of the two children—Albie's mousy and smooth, Flora's blonde and curly. Aggie left nothing out (not even her idea of the real destination of the teapot) except for her seeings. By the Willetts, even if by nobody else, she must be judged for herself alone, not on suspicion of witchcraft.

'I wonder if Mrs Gutteridge knew where the teapot

had gone,' said Mrs Willett. 'She might, you know. And sacked you, Aggie, out of spite; and perhaps to get at her husband sideways.'

'We don't know that, my dear,' said Mr Willett, swallowing tea.

'And now you've heard it all—what's to be done?' Aggie burst out. 'I were going to ask the Osgoods to help me; and perhaps if I could get back to Miss Marriott, she'd give me a bed. But I need a place; and wherever I go, I get thrown out.'

'Not this time,' said Mr Willett. He looked at his wife, over Flora's head; and Aggie saw her nod.

'The Lord has sent you here for a purpose, Aggie,' he said. 'He might have led you to Osgoods', but he didn't: he led you here. My wife and I don't reckon to keep servants, though I have a man and a boy on the farm. But as you can see, my wife and I will have a new little one around May: so my wife would be glad of a hand with the twins, and in the house. We couldn't promise to pay you, but there would be a present for you if the harvest next year turned out good.'

'I could help on the farm, too,' said Aggie, beside herself with relief and pleasure. 'I've helped me dad, when he had piece-work.'

'I'm sure you're a handy girl, Aggie, but I can't have you doing my farm workers out of their jobs,' said Mr Willett. 'You understand about pay?'

'All according to the harvest,' said Aggie.

'Shake hands, then,' said Mr Willett, and they all three shook hands across the willow patterns. Flora and Albie thought it was a game, and shouted; and the cat ran behind the dresser.

Sixteen

'This here ought to be called Hope Farm,' said Aggie to Mrs Willett a few weeks later. 'It's a hopeful place.'

'That's a good name—we might use it. The place runs on hope,' said Mrs Willett, laughing. 'Where you haven't got much money, hope has to do instead.'

'There's more to it than that,' said Aggie. 'You ain't afraid here, are you?'

'Afraid of what?' said Mrs Willett.

'You ain't protected the house, have you?' said Aggie. 'You know—shoes up the chimney, bones under the doorstep.'

'I should think not!' exclaimed Mrs Willett. 'Those are heathenish things. We don't need that sort of tomfoolery, Aggie. God protects us. We do fear God, of course.'

'You mean hell?' said Aggie. 'There's a lot said about hell, in chapel.'

'We don't fear hell, Aggie,' said Mrs Willett. 'Hell is only for the wicked. We need only fear offending God's love.'

I wonder, thought Aggie, if the people who built this house believed that. Or might there be a few somethings hidden away in the walls, that the Willetts never suspected?

Aggie had rapidly realized that her status in her new post was not strictly that of a maid—with employers who kept her at a distance and assumed she was a different order of being. The Willetts believed that all human beings were equal; moreover they and Aggie were all chapelgoers together and, as Mr Willett put it, 'bound up together in the bundle of life'. At chapel

Aggie heard her master and mistress addressed as Brother Joseph and Sister Ruth. On the other hand, there was a difference in age and in knowledge. In the first few days she was there a comfortable compromise had been reached. Aggie called her employers Mr Joseph and Mrs Ruth; she ate her meals with them when the children ate with them, the logic being that she helped to feed the children; but she spent her evening leisure and ate her supper on her own, either in the warmth of the kitchen or in her own little room. After supper she joined the Willetts at their sitting-room fire for Bible study and prayers. The Willetts discussed the Biblical passages they read in the minutest detail, always asking how the words applied to themselves. They don't half take it serious, thought Aggie. Like it was life or death. But there, that's just what they think it is.

Her room was, again, an attic, but Aggie thought it must be the prettiest attic in the world. It was very plainly furnished, with bare boards for flooring with a few rag rugs; but so were all the bedrooms, and Aggie's furniture was no worse than the Willetts' in their own room. She had two windows, facing south and west, and against the south wall was espaliered a pear tree which surrounded that window with a network of twigs.

Aggie was also given her share of leisure time, and enjoyed visits to the Osgoods' house and walks with Hester and Miriam. Part of her job was looking after the twins and taking them for walks around the village in their big hooded pram. 'Willetts' Aggie' became known around the streets and in the shop, and 'Willetts' Aggie' she was happy to be.

Some jobs in the house became exclusively hers— especially the heavier ones, churning, the carrying of slops and fetching of water and scrubbing of brick floors, and the pounding of clothes in the weekly wash.

But most work was shared between her and Mrs Ruth.

On one of the Sundays when it was her turn to go to chapel while Mrs Ruth stayed at home with the twins, she had fitted in a hurried visit to her grandmother. Gran surprised her with a piece of news.

'I saw young Sam, Aggie,' said Gran. 'Yesterday as ever was. He came in to town with a farmer—'

'Bert Syme,' Aggie put in eagerly.

'I daresay,' said Gran. 'He asked in the market and found his way here—quicker than you did, I'll lay. He's sharp, young Sam.'

'What did he say?' demanded Aggie. 'How's me mam, and how's Sam himself?'

'He never said,' said Gran. 'So all right, I suppose. He came for news of you, gal. He'll come again another Saturday.'

'Tell him I'm well fixed, in Hardingley, Gran,' said Aggie. 'A good place with kind people, and little 'uns to look after. I don't get regular pay but I'll get a share of the profits, come harvest.'

'You never told me that,' said Gran. 'No pay—you're a fool, Aggie Flack. They ought to pay you.'

'It's all agreed—I put me hand to it,' said Aggie. 'It's a contract.'

'Fiddle, more like,' said Gran. 'Fiddle, if I ever heard one.'

'Mr Joseph wouldn't do anything unfair,' said Aggie. 'It's all above board, and you can tell Sam so.'

'I'll be telling Sam what I think, not what you think,' said Gran; and there Aggie had to leave it.

After this conversation, Aggie lost her brightness for a few days. She was upset that the Willetts, whom she loved like family, should be suspect; and wondered whether Sam would keep the message for Mam only. What Sam knew, might not Dad find out? To crown her unease she had another seeing—in, of all things, a bucket of water. She had just filled the bucket from the rainwater butt and was looking into it to make sure there were no leaves or living creatures swimming its surface. The surface was unbroken, and in it she saw the door of the cottage at home and herself, luggage in hand, going in at it. She felt herself go red with agitation, and tears come into her eyes; and like this Mrs Ruth found her.

'Where's that water, Aggie?' said Mrs Ruth. 'The copper's hotting up and the washing's waiting.' And then, 'Mercy, child—what is it? What's the matter?'

Aggie was too shaken by the recent seeing to watch her tongue.

'I saw me home, Mrs Ruth, and meself there,' said Aggie. 'And I daresay it's wicked, but I don't want to go back there—I don't!'

'Saw where, Aggie? What do you mean?' asked Mrs Ruth; and Aggie had to explain—the seeings, Bowleses' baby, Mrs Lamb, everything.

Mrs Ruth looked troubled and serious. 'I don't know what to make of this, Aggie,' she said. 'I think it's divination, and that's a branch of witchcraft.'

'But I'm chapel, Mrs Ruth,' said Aggie. 'I don't do witchcraft. I don't know how. What I see, I never ask for.'

'I'll have to talk to Joseph about it,' said Mrs Ruth. 'Now, tip this water in the copper and get some more from the butt. And don't look at it.'

After Bible study and prayers that evening, Mr Joseph gave Aggie a lecture on the subject.

'This seeing, Aggie,' he said. 'It's against Scripture and you will have to fight against it. I understand you don't will it to happen: but what you've got to do is to will it not to happen. When you feel it come on, say your prayers. Say "Our Father". Stop it happening.'

'It's not like that, though,' said Aggie, deeply distressed. 'I don't feel it coming. It's sudden-like. I just see.'

'We will all pray for you,' said Mr Joseph. 'And you pray too—every night. I won't make threats, but I don't see how I can keep a diviner under my roof.'

Aggie went to bed thoroughly miserable and said no prayers at all; but muttered into her pillow, 'I won't go back, I won't . . . But whether I'm there or here, mayn't I be turned out all over again, and called witchy?'

Nothing more was said about Aggie's seeings, by either Mr Joseph or Mrs Ruth, except obliquely in evening prayers. She kept her eyes out of buckets and began to forget her fears. All the same, when a knock came at the front door at mid-morning, two weeks later, she went to answer it with foreboding; and was only half surprised when there on the doorstep of Hope Farm she saw Dad.

SEVENTEEN

The first thing she thought was, He's smaller; I'm near as tall as he is. Or was he always that little? Have I growed?

She said nothing at all, just looked at him.

Dad seemed embarrassed, and so inclined to bluster.

'I'm come for you, Aggie Flack,' he said. 'Your mam ain't too good, and she needs you; and you got to come home.'

'You turned me out,' said Aggie, stony-faced but with her fingers gripped against her palms. 'You said, it weren't my home no more and you wouldn't have me in the house.'

'Maybe I did,' mumbled Dad; and then, gathering energy, 'and what I said, I said right. But that were then, this is now; that talk in the village, that's all died down. Your mam's real poorly, and that alters things. And'—he added in a growl—'if you're working for no money, you can work for me for no money, not some jumped-up chapelgoer.'

So that's it, thought Aggie. I said too much and Sam said too much, and Dad thinks I'm getting no pay here and he'll never stand for that.

Before she could reply—before she even knew how she could reply—Mrs Ruth came up the passageway to the front door with Flora in her arms; Albie could be heard close behind, banging the wall with a wooden spoon.

'What's all this, Aggie?' said Mrs Ruth coolly. 'Who is our visitor?'

'It's me dad, Mrs Ruth,' said Aggie, feeling tearful at the prospect of sympathy. 'He says me mam's poorly and I got to go home; he says, when he turned me out that weren't for ever.'

'I see,' said Mrs Ruth, and spoke to Dad, who stood glowering but silent. 'You have rights over her as her father, Mr Flack,' she said. 'But my husband and I are Aggie's employers, and we shall require some notice. As you see, I have children to care for.' Albie had come stumping up and was tugging at her skirt.

'Where there's no pay, there can't be no employment,' said Mr Flack, finding his sullen tongue. 'I come to fetch her, and I'll fetch her now.'

'That is employment!' Aggie butted in. 'I get me share at harvest. If you let me stay till harvest, there'll be something in it for me.'

Dad looked hesitant. But truth was more important to Mrs Ruth than a convenient half-truth. 'Well, we hope there will be, Aggie,' she said. 'But if the harvest's poor, it may be little enough.'

'Like I said,' said Dad. 'A half-promise, that's all that is. Funny kind of employment.'

'I daresay,' said Mrs Ruth. 'It was a funny situation when we took your daughter to work here. She was homeless when we took her in; and you best know why that was.'

'I changed me mind,' said Dad, sticking to his guns. 'Things is different, and I want her back.'

'My husband is her legal employer,' said Mrs Ruth. 'She can't break her service without his knowing of it. I'll speak to him tonight and we will make arrangements to send her back to you. My husband will write to you and your wife to notify you of when to expect her.'

'I reckoned on taking her back now,' said Dad, a whining tone coming into his voice. 'Her mam needs her.'

'So do I,' said Mrs Ruth, and with some reason—Albie was now shouting and kicking to get her attention, and Flora—who had taken a dislike to Dad—was crying heartily. 'We'll write to you, Mr Flack. And now, good day to you.'

Aggie leapt to the door and shut it firmly before Dad could reply; she heard him kick the front gate as he departed.

'Oh, Mrs Ruth, shall I really have to go?' she said when they had quieted the children and were back in the kitchen together.

'I'm afraid so, Aggie,' said Mrs Ruth. 'We'll see what Joseph says—he'll be in to his dinner soon. But at your age, your parents have control of you. What do you think—is your mother really ill?'

'She might be,' said Aggie. 'She has the Fen Ague, times, like so many do. Or it could be just a tale of Dad's, to get me away from you.'

'How will your father have got here?' said Mrs Ruth as she rocked Flora, while Aggie held a mug of milk to Albie's mouth.

'Walked from Marksey, most like,' said Aggie. 'He'll have to look slippy if he means to go back with Bert Syme.'

'That would have been a horrid long walk for you, Aggie,' said Mrs Ruth. 'I'd have stopped that, anyway. Joseph will take you, when you go.'

'So I'm going,' said Aggie, unable to suppress a sniff.

'I don't see us being able to stop it,' said Mrs Ruth. 'Won't you be glad to be back with your mother, and the other children?'

'I want me mam, right enough,' said Aggie. 'And Sam, I'll be glad to see Sam. But Melia won't want me back there, she won't; and most of them think I'm a witch.'

'If you know you're not, your conscience is clear,' said Mrs Ruth.

But Aggie was still worried, and all the more so when

Mr Joseph came home and gave it as his opinion that she would have to return to her parents.

'Don't look so downcast,' he said. 'You're in God's hands. And if Providence brings you back to Hope Farm—and if, of course, we haven't taken on other help in the meantime—we shall be glad to have you back on the old arrangement. I'll write to your father and say we'll send you back a week tomorrow—that'll be Saturday—and that I'll drive you over. You'll have worked your week's notice. And I'll give you some cash in hand, as you won't be staying till harvest.'

'Don't tell me dad you're doing that, Mr Joseph,' said Aggie. 'He'd have that for his beer money, if you did. If I just take it in me pocket it can go to help me mam.'

'Just as you think,' said Mr Joseph; but Mrs Ruth added, 'Keep a little for yourself. For emergencies.'

The week went all too quickly for Aggie, and she didn't succeed in not being downcast when the day came for her return. She cried at saying goodbye to Mrs Ruth, and cried over the children; but to be driven off in Mr Joseph's smart trap, with his brown cob Sampson between the shafts, was so enjoyable that she let the wind dry the tears off her face and almost smiled at the countryside jigging by.

'Put me down here, Mr Joseph,' said Aggie at the end of the cottage's muddy path. 'Don't come no nearer. If you do and me dad asks about money, you'll tell him the truth.'

'Oh, Aggie, Aggie!' said Mr Joseph, with a shake of his head and a smile. 'You know better, yourself, than to tell lies.'

'What I know and what I do ain't always the same, Mr Joseph,' said Aggie. 'One thing I do know and I can do, though—that's keep me mouth shut.'

'I was going to ask if they'd sometimes let you come

to chapel,' said Mr Joseph. 'I couldn't fetch you every week—but sometimes, on a fine day.'

'Don't ask,' said Aggie shortly. 'Me dad's against religion, and me mam's church. If I ever see me way to coming, I'll get word to you—by Gran, or somehow. I'll try, but I got no hopes.'

'We'll meet again, Aggie,' said Mr Joseph. 'Hope Farm's always there, if you need a refuge again.'

Aggie waved once, then turned and stumped up the path to the cottage, jumping the worst puddles. The cottage door did not open to welcome her, and more and more she wondered what sort of greeting she would get inside.

EIGHTEEN

Just as Dad looked smaller, so did the cottage look smaller. Aggie elbowed the door open and saw a dismal picture. Mam sat, eyes closed, in the high-backed chair near the hearth that was always 'Mam's chair'; her feet were in ashes and the fire unlit, although it was a day of sharp cold. Unwashed crocks from breakfast were still on the table. There was no sign of Dad, or of either of the other children.

'Mam!' whispered Aggie, uncertain whether she was doing right to interrupt her mother's sleep.

Mam's eyes opened and she struggled to sit up straighter.

'Why, Aggie!' she said, her voice shaky. 'I didn't know you was coming today. Your dad said he'd get word when you was coming.'

'Mr Willett sent a letter,' said Aggie. 'To you both. Didn't you get it?'

'Your dad may have seen it. I didn't,' said Mam.

Aggie went and kissed her mother, afraid to hug her too hard—she looked pale and heavy and, to Aggie's eyes, like a suet pudding propped up. She was white-pale, her features pinched and her skin shrunken.

'Where's everybody?' Aggie asked, hanging her coat and hat on the back of the door.

'Your dad never came home last night,' said Mam. 'He'll be lying drunk somewhere. Sam's gone to see if he can get an eel or two for our dinner. Melia's gone to the shop for errands. We're out of matches. She's a long time about it.'

Chattering somewhere, thought Aggie, as she settled down to clear the ashes of yesterday's fire.

'What ails you, Mam?' she said as she shovelled and swept. 'Fen Ague?'

'Ah, and it's a bad go,' said Mam. 'Some days it ain't so bad, but today's terrible.'

'Go back to bed,' urged Aggie. 'I can manage, now I'm here.'

'I'll be better by the fire, when that's lit,' said Mam.

'There'll be matches upstairs, surely,' said Aggie, and hurried off to look; and sure enough, there were matches by her parents' bedroom candle.

As Aggie came down with these, Melia burst in at the door, lively and smiling, a bag of shopping clutched at knee level. The smile went when she saw Aggie.

'Oh, so you're back,' she said. 'Well, if you are, you can do the work, can't you. Can I go and play, then, Mam?'

Anger flared up in Aggie. So she had been dragged back from her happiness and usefulness at Hope Farm in order to release Melia for a longer time of carefree childhood. What about her own childhood—ended so abruptly by Dad in that room less than three months ago?

Melia saw the anger. Her own face paled and her eyes widened in fear. 'Don't witch me, Aggie,' she said. 'Don't put the eye on me!'

'Get off and play, daftie,' said Aggie. 'That's what you want. And don't be stupid. I ain't no witch, so don't tell no stories.'

Melia dropped the shopping and slammed the house door behind her. Aggie knelt down and put a match to the sticks under the new fire. A few tears of misery and self-pity tickled her face and she licked them off, and then went to wash her dirty hands and the breakfast crocks together. Mam was asleep.

She got a better welcome from Sam when he came home in the early afternoon, bringing not eels but a couple of snipe.

77

'Oh good, Ag, you're home,' he said. 'We'll get a real good supper off these birds. I'll pluck them and get the innards out; I know how.'

'You never shot them yourself?' said Aggie.

''Course not—I ain't got no gun,' said Sam. 'Some chaps out on the washes with guns and a young dog; the dog didn't fetch all they brought down, so I got a couple. Dad's out there too, with his gun; we may get some more for the pot when he gets home.'

While Mam slept by the fire and Sam bolted bread and a raw onion, Aggie and he exchanged news. Sam was eager to hear all about Hope Farm and he whispered news to Aggie which put a worried frown on her face.

'Dad's carrying on with that Eliza Goose,' he said. 'Sometimes when Mam thinks he's drunk, he's really round at hers. He sleeps there, too, a night or two a week—that is, if her mam don't find him there and set up a screeching till he goes. But keep it dark. Mam don't know and Melia don't know. Keep it dark, Aggie.'

'Mam ought to be told,' whispered Aggie doubtfully.

'Not while she's ill,' Sam answered. 'When these shakes have gone off we'll tell her. And—' He lowered his voice to a mumble. '—talking of Mam, how come she's got money?'

'She does sewing for folks,' said Aggie, also very softly. 'She gave me some money when I went; I still got a bit.'

'It's in that box where she's got her needles and cottons; it's got like a pretend bottom and that lifts out and she's got money underneath,' said Sam.

'If you ain't the world's nosy parker, Sam Flack!' said Aggie, and Sam winked.

Aggie dropped her voice again. 'You ain't told Melia?' she whispered. 'Well, don't. I don't know what to make of Melia, Sam, but I know she can't keep secrets.'

'She's a rum old girl,' said Sam. 'She's frit of you, Aggie; she don't want you here.'

'So I noticed,' said Aggie. 'She'll have to make the best of it. Get on then, get them birds plucked; I'll get the pot on.'

When Dad came in, wet and hungry from the wetlands, his gun over his arm and Piper at his heels, there was a good smell of cooking in the cottage. He gave Aggie no greeting, only said, 'Where's me dinner, then, gal?'

'Did you know I were coming today?' Aggie asked him. 'Did you get a letter?'

'A letter come,' said Dad.

'Didn't you give it to Mam to read?' Aggie asked.

Dad gave her a meaning look, and she remembered the weight of his hand. 'What matter? She knows now,' was all he said.

He ate well from the stew, and so did Melia when she came home.

Aggie knew she ought to watch her tongue but she couldn't resist whispering, 'Witch food ain't so bad, hey, Melia?'

Melia dropped her spoon and gave Aggie a look of horror.

'Don't be daft,' said Aggie, still in a low tone. 'I'm pulling your leg. I don't know witchcraft and all I cook is ordinary vittles.'

'I've finished,' said Melia, pushing her bowl away, a scowl on her face.

'I'll see if Mam can eat some more,' said Aggie. She took Melia's dish and offered it to Mam. Mam seemed hardly to have the power to feed herself, and did best if Aggie spooned food into her as she had done with Flora and Albie at Hope Farm. After this Aggie helped her mother up to bed, and when she came down found Dad, Sam, and Piper asleep by the fire (Sam lying with Piper on the rug, a tangled bundle of legs and paws) and Melia washing dishes.

'I'm sorry I teased, Melia,' said Aggie. 'We got to live together in one house, and that's a little one, so we'd better get on. I won't tease no more, but don't act like you're scared of me. I never done you—or anyone else—no harm, and I won't start now. If I could, I wouldn't; and I can't.'

Melia kept her back to Aggie, and sniffed as tears ran down her thin face. 'I won't sleep in one bed with you, Aggie Flack,' she said. 'I daren't.'

Aggie was flummoxed. 'We got to, Melia,' she said. 'Mam wouldn't want you should share with Sam, and you can't sleep on the floor.'

'I'll grow twisted,' sniffed Melia. 'Old Matty's twisted. That's what witchcraft does to you.'

'She'd never have done it to herself,' said Aggie. 'Don't talk so woolly. If you're frit, put some safety leaves under your pillow—yarrow, groundsel, holly. Any of them leaves will do.'

'Ain't no leaves on them now,' said Melia with a sob. 'Only holly. I'll get holly.'

Aggie was shocked to sense how real and deep Melia's fear was, but could see a gleam of humour in the idea of herself teaching Melia charms against her own supposed power.

'All right then,' was all she said. 'And put your shoes under the bed, tonight.'

Melia nodded, silent.

Aggie went up later to check that Mam was asleep, and carried Mam's candle into the children's room. Out of curiosity she looked inside the bed she and Melia would be sharing. Down the middle of it, between her side and Melia's side, a row of holly twigs was laid. Pinned to Melia's skimpy nightdress was a bedraggled knot of red ribbon (also a charm against bewitchment) and under Melia's pillow was a stone with a hole through it. People used these stones both to keep witches away and to keep off cramp; Aggie knew what Melia's was for. It hardly looked as though she was in for a happy time at home.

NINETEEN

The next day, when the younger ones had been fed and had gone out and Mam had been given her porridge and persuaded to stay in bed for a time, Aggie did a quick clean round the downstairs room and then sat by the glowing turf to think. Mam was ill; Mam needed medical help. Dad would never stir himself to do anything for her; Sam, though sensible, was too young to take responsibility, and help from Melia out of the question. She would have to take action herself. There was only Dr Mortlock to turn to, and he lived in Fen Deeping (where the school was). He would ask for money—but she had some money, and Mam herself had more. She determined to go next day and request a call from him; and she went upstairs to tell Mam so.

Mam was getting up, and Aggie helped her into her dress and shawl before she told her about her decision.

'Lord's sake, Aggie!' said Mam. 'Don't waste your money, and I won't waste mine. You know what Dr Mortlock's like. What's the use?'

'Is he always drunk, then?' said Aggie.

'It ain't drink,' said Mam. 'It's the stuff—the stuff folks take for the ague. He's fair hooked on it; he takes it all the time. Most days, he's more asleep than awake. That gets you, that does; and that's got Dr Mortlock good and proper. I don't want to start taking that stuff, that I don't.'

'How does he do his job if he's squiffy?' asked Aggie.

'Badly, that's how,' said Mam. 'Half the time, Eliza Goose does it for him.'

Aggie laced up Mam's boots, digesting this information. Eliza Goose, she knew, was taking over

82

from her ageing and arthritic mother the job of village 'handywoman'—who helped at births, attended deathbeds, and laid out corpses ready for burial. Aggie could remember seeing Eliza sometimes riding in Dr Mortlock's trap with him, and coming with him out of houses where somebody was mortally ill.

'Then what if I ask Miss Goose about your ague?' she asked.

'I won't have you go near her, Aggie,' said Mam emphatically. 'You're old enough to know what's what, and you should know what all the village knows—Eliza's not a good woman, nor she ain't a kind one. She carries on with men—half the men in the village, if all that's told about her's true. And if all that's told about him's true, that Dr Mortlock's one of them.'

'I don't like you to be ill and no help given you,' said Aggie, sniffing back tears.

'Get helping, then,' said Mam. 'There's the dinner to get on.'

Next morning, Aggie walked the two miles and a bit to Dr Mortlock's and rang the bell at his front door.

'If it's for the doctor, he can't see anyone,' said a crabby-looking woman at his door. 'He ain't well.'

Ah, and I know why, thought Aggie. Aloud she said, 'Can I leave a message?'

'I suppose so; but I can't promise he'll come,' said the woman—presumably Dr Mortlock's housekeeper or maid. She hadn't the look of a wife.

'Then please will he call at Flacks' cottage, next to Bowleses' that used to be a farm,' said Aggie. 'Me mam's ill.'

'Is she dying?' asked the woman.

'Cor blast, I hope not,' said Aggie. 'She got the Fen Ague—you don't die of that, do you?'

'You do,' said the woman. 'In the end. Write your name on here, then, and I'll see he gets it. There ain't no saying when he'll come, and if she ain't dying, maybe he won't.'

Aggie wrote 'Flack—by Bowleses—Fen Ague—bad' on the large slate the woman gave her, and muttered a disgusted 'Goodnight!' as she banged the doctor's gate.

Two days went by, with no sign of the doctor; and Aggie couldn't decide whether to try him again or whether to give him up as a lost cause. She didn't tell her mother she had asked him to call; and she didn't tell her mother when she made her next move, which was to visit Eliza Goose.

It was a bright, blowy day when she went to the Goose house and she was not surprised to see Eliza out in her garden spreading washing to dry on her row of currant-bushes. Aggie grinned to herself as Miss Goose snatched a pair of bloomers off a bush and tucked them modestly into her basket.

I wonder she cares, if she's going with half the men like they say, thought Aggie.

'You want me, or you want my mother?' asked Eliza Goose, sharp and unfriendly.

'You and your mother both,' said Aggie. 'I want advising.'

'Come into the house, then,' said Eliza grudgingly. She led Aggie into a room rather bigger than the downstairs room in the Flack cottage. Old Mrs Goose sat by the fire, knitting with twisted hands; by her side sat her son, Eliza's younger brother, playing with his own fingers like a baby. He was a man whose brain had never developed fully and who needed help with almost everything he did.

'Morning, Mrs Goose, Mr Goose,' said Aggie.

'Luke Goose,' said the man, brightening up at the chance to show he knew his name.

The old lady said nothing, only nodded and counted her stitches out loud.

'Spit it out, then, Aggie Flack,' said Eliza.

'It's me mam, Mrs Goose,' said Aggie. 'She's poorly with the ague.'

'Get the doctor, then,' Eliza put in.

'I asked him, but he never came,' said Aggie. 'You both know about illness. The old girl at the doctor's, she said you could die of Fen Ague. I want to know, can you die; and what should I do?'

'You can die,' said Mrs Goose, smiling as if the thought pleased her. 'Old or young, you can die.'

' 'Course you can die,' said Eliza, rather more loudly. 'Keep her warm and feed her well and give her poppy if you can get it.'

'She don't want poppy,' began Aggie.

'She can suit herself, then,' said Eliza. 'Unless there's something more you know about, yourself.'

She said this with a sidelong smile that Aggie did not like. Aggie felt her face go hot, and clenched her hands together. Eliza meant witchcraft; Eliza meant to tease and embarrass her. Aggie knew she should not rise to the bait. 'Is that all you can say?' she demanded.

'All the advice we can give. And we want paying for it,' said Eliza.

'Paying!' said Aggie aghast. Neighbours usually helped each other any way they could in the village, and payment was never mentioned. 'I got no money on me,' she added.

'I don't mean money,' said Eliza. 'You can sit with Luke an hour while I take me mother round to Bowleses'. She likes a little talk with Lilian Bowles, Mam does; but we can't leave Luke alone, nor we can't take him where he ain't welcome.'

'All right,' said Aggie. She felt sympathy for Luke, and knew how to entertain him. 'Give me a bit of string, then, Mrs Goose; and I'll sit.'

So while the Goose ladies went on their call, Aggie kept Luke in cheerful laughter by showing him cat's cradles—all the ones she knew, several times over—and singing him the playground songs that he liked but could neither understand nor remember. It was much more than an hour before his mother and sister got home.

'That's it, then,' said Aggie to herself as she toasted a little bit of cheese to tempt Mam to eat. 'I tried the doctor, and I tried the handywoman; all that's left me to try is the witch.'

TWENTY

Aggie had never been to Old Matty's house—never so much as looked in the windows. The schoolchildren usually hurried past with their fingers crossed, looking away from the house rather than at it, and perhaps spitting on the roadway as they passed. Even going on a virtuous errand, like today's, she thought she had better protect herself. 'In the name of the Father, Son, and Holy Ghost,' she said as she stood outside the rickety door. She gave the door a determined rap, then backed nervously away.

She had a long wait before the door was opened; even then it was only pulled ajar and a suspicious face appeared in the crack.

With an effort of memory Aggie came up with Old Matty's proper name.

'Can I talk to you, Mrs Abbs?' she said. 'Can I come in?'

Matty Abbs jerked the door fully open and Aggie, who had come close and had been clutching at the handle, almost fell into the cottage. She stood twisting her fingers together and looking timidly around her.

'Take a good look,' said Matty sharply.

'It's lovely,' said Aggie. 'I never thought it would be so nice.'

'So clean, you mean,' said Matty, and grinned. 'I were never married, Aggie Flack, though I take the title; but I'm a good housewife.'

The cottage inside was neat and comfortable. Aggie looked at everything—swept hearth, glowing peat, polished brass and copper pans; and bunches of herbs hung from the central beam. Bowleses' cat lay asleep by the fire, on a hooked rug bright with patterns. And while Aggie looked around, Matty looked attentively at her, with pale grey eyes that had a dark ring round the iris.

Finally Aggie looked back at the old woman and smiled an embarrassed smile as she met that calm gaze.

'Sit down, then,' said Matty, and pointed to a three-legged stool between the fire and the table. 'And tell me your trouble. I suppose it's a child.'

'No, it ain't!' exclaimed Aggie. 'I'm not growed up yet, I can't have a child.'

'What, then?' said Matty. She sat the other side of the table and Aggie stared straight into those odd eyes, and took in too the heavily wrinkled but shiny-clean face; the rat's-tail dark grey hair falling free of its knot; the twisted shoulder that gave the effect of a hump; and the shabby but well-washed black clothes. 'What can I tell you that you can't see?' added Matty.

Aggie caught her breath in a gasp but decided to ignore the inner meaning of this remark—if there was one.

'It's me mam, Mrs Abbs,' she said. 'Fen Ague, and it's bad. Dr Mortlock won't come and Eliza Goose won't say nothing; and Mam don't get no better. Can you give me something: to swallow, or to say?'

Old Matty grinned at her. 'Ain't you gone chapel?' she said.

Aggie went fiercely red. 'Yes, and I said prayers for her, and will do,' she said.

'Prayer's powerful,' said Matty. 'But you'd like to come at it both ways—hedge your bets, like? Is that it?'

'I'm not silly, Mrs Abbs,' said Aggie.

Matty cackled with laughter and Aggie found herself liking, even trusting, this dangerous woman whom half the village hated and all the village feared.

'Well, then,' said Matty. 'I'll give you herbs. Feverfew,

for one; but I won't tell you all of them. Knowing's knowing.'

'And something to say?' said Aggie.

'I'll do the saying while I blend the herbs,' said Matty. 'You stick to your prayers, Aggie Flack.'

Aggie sat silent while Matty chopped and crumbled dried leaves, and powdered them with a pestle; Matty muttered inaudibly as she worked and Aggie prayed in her head.

'One thing I'll tell you,' said Matty as she emptied the mixture into what looked to Aggie like an old tobacco tin. 'Your mam's in danger.'

'You mean the ague? She might die?' asked Aggie, in alarm.

'I mean something else,' said Matty. 'I don't know for sure what that is. You're the looker: you look.'

She poured some water from a jug into a deep basin and held it out to Aggie.

Aggie shook her head vigorously. 'It's divination,' she said. 'The Bible's against it.'

'Cor blast, if you ain't a daft lummox,' said Matty. 'Where do you think gifts come from, child? I'm a-giving you good warning: take a look, and take thought.'

Aggie stood the basin on the table and looked fearfully into the water. As it stilled, her own face, broken by the movement of the shaken surface, was lost and another picture came into view. She saw the heads and shoulders of her father and Eliza Goose, who were standing close together. Eliza, slightly the taller of the two, had her hands on Dad's shoulders; the two were smiling—a smile that seemed to hold complicity, to hold something threatening. Moreover, Eliza Goose was wearing Mam's shawl, Mam's favourite garment. It had a vivid Paisley pattern in red and brown, and had been a present from Mam's sister, Aunt Jane, before Dad had quarrelled with Aunt Jane and had ordered her not to visit any more.

Aggie did not understand what she saw; and she turned to Matty in bafflement and confusion, rubbing her eyes as normal vision returned.

'I can't make it out,' she complained.

'Think it over,' urged Old Matty. 'And tell your mam.'

'How do you know what I saw?' Aggie asked.

'I don't,' said Matty. 'But I know human nature. "The wicked worketh a deceitful work"; you can find that in the Bible. Likewise, that's common sense.'

'All right then,' said Aggie. She felt shaken and absent, as she often did after a seeing. 'I'll think, and I'll tell Mam. Shall I go now?'

'One thing you can do first,' said Matty.

'Pay you—I know. I got money,' said Aggie. She had come prepared this time.

'Do me a service,' said Matty. 'It's worth more than money.'

Aggie laughed, and felt comfortable with herself again.

'That's what them Gooses wanted,' she said. 'I'll help you, Mrs Abbs. What with?'

'Stir this,' said Old Matty. She went to the little black pot hanging on its hook above her fire, lifted it down and stood it in the hearth. A smell of dried rose petals and something more tangy—verbena, Aggie thought—came from it.

'Is it a love charm?' Aggie asked.

'Ask no questions, then you can't answer if you're asked,' said Matty.

'But why me?' Aggie demanded. Matty Abbs was spry for her eighty-odd years, in spite of her hunched shoulder. If she could keep her cottage bright she could certainly stir a pot.

'For because you're a young maid ain't never been with a man,' said Old Matty. 'That gives you special power. You ain't been with no fellow, have you?'

''Course I ain't,' said Aggie, turning red. 'But I can't rightly do it, Mrs Abbs. Ain't it magic? Ain't it wicked?'

'Stirring ain't magic,' said Matty.

'Can I say a prayer while I stir?' Aggie asked.

'Say what you like,' said Matty.

So Aggie, torn between good manners and a fear of the hell of the wicked, stirred the little pot and prayed for love, marriage, and happiness for any girl who drank the mixture—in the name of the Father, Son, and Holy Ghost.

She went home with her tobacco tin and with a very tangled mind; and that afternoon she gave Mam a tea made of the herbs and told her about her seeing.

Mam made no objection to drinking Mrs Abbs's medicine. 'She knows herbs, Old Matty, like Granny Flack does,' said Mam. 'She's a good friend when she's a friend: but don't ever you cross her, Aggie. She'd be a bad enemy.'

And to Aggie's description of her vision Mam said only, 'I hear you, Aggie; you done right to tell me. From now on, you make all my food and drink yourself—see to it. And tell me anything you hear about your dad and Eliza Goose.'

'Sam says they're going together and half the village knows,' Aggie blurted out.

'Ah. And I know, and all,' said Mam. 'Be watchful, Aggie; that's all I say.'

In spite of the warm fire and the hot drink, Mam shivered and her skin was a yellowy-grey. Aggie suspected that it was not only with the ague, but also with fear.

TWENTY-ONE

There followed for Aggie several anxious weeks. For a time Mam seemed better and brighter; then she had a bad spell with high fever and even vomiting. Aggie watched her protectively while contriving to keep Dad and the children fed and the house cleaned: the younger ones helped—Melia not without grumbling. Dad as usual did nothing in the house except shout for what he wanted and shout when he didn't like what he got (which included, sometimes, Aggie's cooking). He seemed, however, quieter than he often was. Aggie thought that he was living with a secret excitement and put it down to his adventures with Eliza Goose.

At last came a dreadful few days when Mam suffered violent sickness and diarrhoea and Aggie needed to be more a nurse than a housekeeper. Mam was always in bed. Sam and Melia did the cooking (Dad swore and said it was disgusting) and Aggie ran up and down stairs with slop buckets and clean water and—whenever she could manage it—clean sheets. Life was made harder for her by Melia's whisperings. Melia said to her openly one day, 'Mam got worse since you come home. All the village is saying it. You put bad magic on her, that's what they say.'

Aggie could not cope with this: she leapt at Melia and shook her until Melia screamed and fought free. Melia said nothing else openly, but Aggie was aware of looks askance and things Melia muttered behind her hand. She had no time to go to other houses and find out whether what Melia said was true.

After one bad bout of sickness Mam beckoned Aggie to her and said, under her breath, 'Where do you keep them herbs you got from Matty Abbs?'

'On the shelf by the tea and sugar,' said Aggie, also in a whisper.

'Well, don't use them no more,' said Mam. 'Make me ordinary tea, Aggie, and don't say nothing about it to nobody. Don't let nobody see what you're doing, and throw a pinch or two of herbs away every day. Let them all think it's the herbs I'm drinking.'

'Well, all right,' said Aggie. 'There can't be harm in them herbs, Mam. They done you good, first off.'

'I'm saying nothing, Aggie,' said Mam. 'Just make me ordinary tea.'

Aggie contrived to keep her brew-ups for her mother unseen; and in a few days Mam was remarkably better, coming downstairs again and able to eat—even to do a little sewing.

One day when they were alone and Aggie saw Mam's fingers dipping into her sewing box, she remembered Sam's secret. In the present anxious atmosphere in the house, she felt that secrets could only be a bad thing.

'Mam,' she said, her voice low. 'Sam knows you've got money in that box. If he knows, anyone could know. You best hide it somewhere else.'

'Ah, I best had,' said Mam, also softly. 'You're a good daughter, Aggie. See that crack, where the plaster shrunk away from the window-frame? There's one like that upstairs, in me and Dad's bedroom. I got some stuff hidden there.'

Aggie took a look for herself when Mam was downstairs and she was cleaning the bedroom. Stuffed into the crack, and hidden by a loose lump of plaster wedged over it, was a substantial packet—most of it money in notes, tied with a piece of string. Aggie felt relief that Mam, so hedged about with difficulties and—it seemed—dangers, had resources of her own.

It must have been another three weeks before Mam was taken severely ill again—weeks in which she seemed gradually to pick up strength, although not without setbacks. Aggie began to feel hopeful and, now that she was not so tied by nursing, to make a few visits. To her relief, people greeted her normally. Melia's suspicions seemed to be Melia's own.

She did not talk to Old Matty, but she left a bunch of snowdrops at her door. She had a long and cheerful chat with Mam's friend Carrie Bean, and came home with a gift of a jar of calves'-foot jelly for Mam; it was supposed to be a strengthening food for invalids and Carrie knew Mam liked it. Carrie, and a few other friends, called on Mam too, bringing her the village news and gossip.

But a day or two after Aggie's visit to Carrie Mam had another serious setback: again with sickness and fever, and this time even worse than before.

'I'm getting Dr Mortlock,' said Aggie to Dad when he came in from work and the pub.

'No, you ain't,' said Dad. 'He's useless—you know that, gal. He's a poppy-drinker and he ain't fit for his work.'

'We got to do something, Dad,' said Aggie. 'She's that weakly, she might die.'

'I'm the one what decides, Aggie Flack,' said her father. 'I'll get Eliza to come by.'

'Mam don't like Eliza Goose,' protested Aggie.

'Oh? And why not?' said Dad aggressively.

'You know why not,' said Aggie. Dad hit her on the cheek with his open hand, and then made a fist of it; Aggie ducked away to avoid a further blow.

'I said, that's me what decides,' said Dad. He stumped out into the darkness and the door banged after him.

Aggie thought it better not to alarm Mam, in her feeble state, until the morning—for surely Eliza Goose would not turn out to walk the wet byways until daylight came?

It was to the disgust and misery of all the young Flacks that half an hour later the house door swung open on the rainy night and Dad and Eliza Goose came in together, Eliza carrying a closed lantern and both of them running with water.

'Well, here I am—Nurse Goose!' said Eliza brightly. She got no answer, so went on, 'I'll just show myself upstairs, then, and see the patient. Light me a candle, will you, Noah?'

The young ones noted her use of their father's first name.

'I'll come up with you,' said Aggie.

'No, no—no extra people in the sickroom,' said Eliza. 'That's the first rule. I'll tell you what needs doing when I come down.'

The three young ones looked apprehensively at Eliza when she came down, and didn't like her solemn frown. Dad smiled.

'It's bad news, Noah,' said Eliza heavily. 'Poor Mary ain't just got the Fen Ague, like we thought; she's took the typhus. That's a real bad illness and that spreads like wildfire. I'll move in here and I'll nurse her and please God she'll be spared. But you children, you've got to go, and go sharpish. You can't stay here and risk the typhus too.'

The three just stared at her. Sam was the first to find his tongue.

'It's late, and it's wet as hell,' he said. 'Where do you think we're going to, Miss Goose?'

'Carrie Bean will take the two girls,' said Eliza. 'She's only got the one bed spare, though, and she don't like boys. Maybe the Fitches will take you, Sam.'

Sam brightened visibly. Bob Fitch was his current hero at school.

'I don't like to push off and leave Mam,' said Aggie in real distress. 'I can do what needs to be done, Miss

Goose, if you'll tell me how. Let me stay! Dad, you know I looked after her proper. You'll say I can stay?'

'I say you can't, that's what,' said Dad. 'Eliza's in the right of it. Get the children's things, Aggie, and look slippy about it. You're to be out of here in ten minutes.'

Mam was asleep when Aggie went up. Sobbing as she did so, Aggie tumbled a few things for Melia and herself into the carpet-bag. There was no bag for Sam's, which had to go into a newspaper parcel tied round with knotted-together bootlaces.

When all was such an emergency, and such a rush, Aggie didn't understand why when she and Melia arrived on Carrie Bean's doorstep, dripping rain, Carrie said, 'Come in, girls; your bed's made up,' and why Carrie seemed already to know about typhus and Mam's weak state. Sam had the same experience: welcomed in by the Fitches, but put to sleep alone, on the sofa, 'in case the infection took'.

Who had had foreknowledge, Aggie wondered? Was there someone else in the village who had seeings? Or had Eliza made up her mind in advance what the diagnosis was to be?

These things troubled her as she got ready for bed in a neat white room (and yes, Melia had snatched a piece of holly from a wet hedge for the bed they were going to share). It also worried Aggie that when she thanked Carrie Bean for the calves'-foot jelly and said how Mam had relished it, Carrie answered, 'That's grand, Aggie. I don't make it meself, you know.'

TWENTY-TWO

The next few days were dreadful ones. Sam and Melia were off school, in quarantine; and neither Carrie Bean nor the Fitches wanted children indoors all day. But the weather was going through a dry spell and they were happy enough 'mooching about'—climbing trees, trapping eels, skimming stones on the water. Aggie couldn't settle to join them.

She was pleased when she thought of a useful occupation for herself. If Eliza Goose was at Flacks', nobody was in the Goose cottage to look after old Mrs Goose and Luke. Aggie went round there on the first morning and found a poor state of affairs. Water and peat needed to be fetched; the fire was out, Mrs Goose scolding Luke for being useless and Luke crying because he wanted to go to the privy and his mother wasn't listening to him. Aggie understood his whimpers and led him off outside. Later, she got the fire going and a kettle on it, and got tea made for mother and son.

'She got what she wants, my Lizzie,' said Mrs Goose spitefully as she sipped tea. 'Years she wanted to get out of here and leave us two feeble ones to take care of ourselves; and now she done it.'

'That's only for a few days, Mrs Goose,' said Aggie, chilled to her marrow at what was being suggested. 'My mother will be better and Miss Goose will come back here.'

'Think so, do you?' snorted the old lady. 'All I can say is, you don't know my Lizzie, Aggie Flack. She couldn't get away as a girl by marrying—she never met a man that daft. Till she met Noah Flack.'

'My mam's still there and my dad's married to her,' said Aggie. 'I thought Miss Goose had lots of offers.'

'There's offers and offers. Marriage ain't always one of them,' said Mrs Goose. 'She'd have been a good wife, if she'd ever got down to it. She can nurse, and she cooks lovely; and who's to cook for us now, I'm sure I don't know.'

Aggie did her best by finding bread and cheese and pickle for a mid-day meal for them. Their house had a larder and she was impressed by the jars of jams and chutneys there, and the bunches of herbs as neatly hung as Old Matty's. There were several kinds of pickle and Aggie had to call out to find what kind the Gooses preferred. For her trouble, she was invited to eat with them.

After the early dusk had come Aggie went round to her home and lingered near the back door, wondering about Mam and saying a prayer or two. When Eliza Goose came out to carry slops to the privy, Aggie dodged into the pigsty and waited till she returned. If Eliza had only gone out for longer, Aggie could have slipped inside to see Mam; but there was no chance that day. She went back to Carrie Bean's disconsolate.

The next two days followed the same pattern; and on the last of them, Aggie got inside her own home. She arrived there when dusk was only just falling and found Dr Mortlock's trap outside the cottage door, and lurked in the pigsty, full of fears. By the light of his carriage lamps she saw Dr Mortlock come out, walking unsteadily and steered by Eliza Goose.

'Like I told you, ain't it,' Eliza was saying. 'Clear case of typhus.'

'Yes, indeed, yes,' said Dr Mortlock vaguely. 'Help me back the horse, Eliza.'

Eliza Goose helped him, under Aggie's scornful eye—

I could have done it neater, she thought. Then not only did Eliza help Dr Mortlock into the trap—she got in beside him, and the two drove away.

Eliza had not locked the door, and Aggie shot into the house and up the stairs. She must see Mam, she thought, before Dad got home from work or Eliza Goose got back.

Mam lay apparently asleep, wax-white and thin-faced. The house smelt terrible, Aggie thought: of illness, of vomit and worse. She realized for the first time not only that Mam might die, but that she might die soon.

'Mam,' she whispered tentatively, and Mam's eyes flew open and she managed a smile.

'What did Dr Mortlock say?' asked Aggie.

'Him,' said Mam—her voice for a moment strong enough to show contempt. 'Half-seas over. Typhus, he says; likely to be fatal. If it's typhus, where's me rash?' Her eyes closed again. 'Get me a glass of water, Aggie,' she muttered almost inaudibly.

After she had drunk the water, she seemed to revive a little. 'I'm not always asleep when they think I'm asleep,' she said. 'Don't be surprised at whatever news you hear, Aggie; and don't lose heart. Use your gift, child; look, and don't talk about what you see.'

'What do you mean, Mam?' asked Aggie.

'I can't say no more,' said Mam; and indeed her voice was hardly more than a whisper. 'You'd best go. Don't be frit, Aggie, and don't let the little ones fret. We'll be together again.'

Aggie kissed her, and crept down the stairs; and cried all the way back to Carrie Bean's.

But her restlessness and anxiety were extreme. After supper she told Carrie Bean she wanted to call on the Gooses before she went to bed. She did pass by the Gooses' cottage, but she didn't call; she went on to her own home, put her ear to the crack between the house door and the doorpost, and listened with strained attention.

Dad and Eliza Goose were there. Aggie could hear voices, and a snatch or two of talk. They were near the door, she thought; but not as near as she would have liked.

' . . . see the vicar . . . ' said Eliza's voice.

'Ain't it too soon?' This was Dad's voice.

'Got to give some notice.' Eliza's.

' . . . death sistificate . . . ' Dad's.

'All done by Dr Mortlock!' Eliza's, and a laugh.

'Honest, Eliza, I don't know how you do it!' Dad's; and he laughed too.

Then a gap, while they moved around; then Eliza saying, ' . . . sleep, or a coma', and Dad saying ' . . . go out for a drink—can't do no harm.'

Aggie withdrew into the elder bush by the pigsty and watched as Dad locked the door and he and Eliza went off arm in arm towards the Nag's Head. She tried the door: it was really locked. She called 'Mam!' under the window, but she got no answer. Sleep, or a coma, she thought. God, don't let her die. Please don't let her die.

She went back, snuffling a bit, to Carrie Bean's; and straight up to bed with Melia.

'You smell of witches,' said Melia fearfully. 'Elder tree, witch tree. Where you been—witches' tea-party?'

'I went home,' said Aggie. 'Mam's real ill, Melia, and doctor's been.'

'She won't die, will she?' asked Melia, with a new terror.

'I don't know, Melia, honest,' said Aggie. 'I did get in, this afternoon; she were talking queer.'

'Can't you do some magic?' whined Melia.

'You know I can't,' said Aggie. 'I can say a prayer, and so can you.'

When Aggie got into bed her thoughts would give her no rest. Melia slept, but Aggie turned and twisted. She finally fell into a deep sleep in the small hours, and was still sleeping heavily when Carrie Bean came in, candle in hand, to wake the girls.

'I'm most awful sorry, Aggie, Melia,' she said. 'Your dear mam's dead and gone to rest. She died in the night.'

TWENTY-THREE

Mam's coffin went down into water. The underground water was so near the surface, in the Fens (and especially after a wet winter), that water would start to seep into the bottom of a grave as soon as it was dug. Aggie hated to think of Mam going down into the wet.

Melia stood white-faced and would not look at the grave; Sam, who was desperately afraid of anything to do with death, stood with his eyes shut and his hands made into fists. Dad, showing no expression, threw a handful of wet gritty soil on to the coffin lid by way of leave-taking. Aggie had made a bunch of half-opened violets, the only mourner's flowers Mam had, and threw that down with a whisper of 'Goodbye, Mam!' She remembered her mother's words and thought, We'll be together again—but it was without great conviction. She had not acquired the Willetts' vivid belief in Heaven.

After the funeral and the fumigation of the house which Eliza Goose said she had carried out under Dr Mortlock's instructions, the young Flacks moved back into the cottage. For all their sniffing, they couldn't smell whatever disinfectant the doctor had prescribed. The house smelt faintly of illness and strongly of beer and mutton chops, a dish Eliza was fond of. Aggie made it her business to look in her mother's bedroom, as soon as she got the chance. The money was gone from its hiding-place in the wall; Mam's books were gone, and even the family Bible in which she meant to write the date of Mam's death.

Although there was now no need of her in the cottage, Eliza showed no signs of moving out.

'You've been very kind, Miss Goose,' said Aggie to

her on their second day back in the cottage. 'But I can manage now. Melia and Sam can help me till they go back to school, and I can do the cooking.'

'What I hear, your dad don't fancy your cooking,' said Eliza Goose. She was a big woman, broad and fat, and she loomed over Aggie, staring her out with watery blue eyes. Aggie felt childish and helpless beside her.

'Dad don't need no housekeeper, and he can't pay you, neither,' Aggie persisted.

'He ain't said he don't want me, and I reckon I'll get paid,' said Eliza. She smiled a contented catlike smile and Aggie was silent, hating her.

Next, Aggie tackled Dad. She caught him one day outside the house, where he was cleaning his gun in a streak of morning sunshine.

'Dad, how long is Miss Goose staying?' she asked bluntly. 'I don't need help now, and I don't see how you can afford to pay her.'

Dad grinned at her and took an oily cotton rag out of his jaws, where he had been holding it.

'She'll stay as long as we both fancy it,' he said. 'That's no skin off your nose. Gives you less work to do.'

'What about her old mam, and that Luke?' demanded Aggie.

'Well, what?' said Dad. 'They can fend for theirselves. They got hands, ain't they?'

'Then there's Melia and Sam. She don't get on with them,' said Aggie.

'You mean, they don't get on with her,' said Dad. 'Like it or lump it, all of you. I like her company; she likes mine. She's staying.'

But that's in Mam's bed, thought Aggie as she went back inside. And that's in Mam's best shawl, she might have added. Eliza was now wearing the red Paisley which Mam had so much loved.

For a few weeks there was armed truce in the cottage. Sam and Melia went back to school. Aggie did the housework in grim silence; Eliza cooked. And, to be fair to her, Eliza did make regular visits to her mother's cottage to check on the provisions in the larder and to do a wash. Aggie called round there with a loaf of Eliza's making, one day, and saw a card in Eliza's writing stuck in the window:

FOR HANDYWOMAN, GO TO FLACKS.

She gritted her teeth in annoyance.

The armed truce, however, took a sudden turn for the worse and became less a truce than a campaign of wearing down by Eliza. The helpings of food given to the young people became steadily smaller, until Aggie and Sam, who were hearty eaters, were always ravenous. At the same time, Eliza carried on a battle of words against Sam.

Oddly enough, as it seemed to Aggie, tough Sam who would take on a bigger boy in a playground battle was more vulnerable than Melia. Unkind words bounced off Melia, who merely concentrated on thinking of a vicious reply. Sam withered under sarcasm and would be reduced to near tears by Eliza's bitter remarks.

On his eleventh birthday he did answer Eliza back. Aggie had bought him a dozen marbles and a packet of peppermints, Melia had bought him a penny whistle. Dad had forgotten, of course. Sam had been teased and 'bumped' at school and came home feeling happy and important.

'Oh, so here's the hero home,' said Eliza, as he came in, grinning. 'Fancy ourselves, don't we! Great useless lump.'

'I can leave school when I've passed me exams,' said Sam, avoiding her eye. 'And I can leave here.'

'What you think you'd be good for, I'm sure I don't

know,' said Eliza. 'You're a no-good oaf, Sammy Flack; a real fen potato-head.'

'Sticks and stones, Sam,' said Aggie, seeing him flinch.

'You keep out of it, girl,' said Eliza sharply to Aggie. 'You're as useless as he is.'

'Not when it comes to cooking,' said Aggie. 'Sam, I made you a cake.'

Sam looked up, brightening.

'Cake! What cake?' demanded Eliza. There was a nasty gleam of triumph in her eye that struck Aggie with alarm.

'I made it when you went to your mother's,' said Aggie. 'It's in the tin.'

Eliza snatched the lid off the tin. Inside was a lump of black peat off the cottage's fuel stack.

Aggie and Melia stared; Sam burst into tears and ran out of the house.

'What did you do with it?' asked Melia. Aggie was wordless with anger and concern for Sam.

'Took it round to Bowleses' pig. That weren't fit for humans to eat,' said Eliza, smiling her hard smile.

'What is there for tea, then?' said Melia.

'I've no idea. You'd best look,' said Eliza.

While Melia cut up half a stale loaf, Aggie went out and found Sam crying wretchedly in the pigsty.

'Don't mind it, Sam,' urged Aggie. 'Don't give her the satisfaction. She don't matter. She ain't like a real person.'

'She lives in our house,' sobbed Sam, only half coherent. 'She sleeps where our mam slept. What's more, Aggie, I don't think Mam died natural. Who's to say that precious pair didn't do her in? I won't stay here—I won't! I'll run away.'

'You need to finish the year at school,' said Aggie persuasively.

'No, I don't,' said Sam. 'I'm a quick learner. I learned all Miss Reeves knows, long ago. I'm best in the school at sums. I'm better'n she is.'

'Aggie!' came a sharp voice out of the cottage door. 'Aggie! Where are you, gal? The water needs fetching.'

'Coming!' called Aggie. She gave Sam a brief hug and went for the bucket.

Her mind was full of Sam and his agonies, and without thinking she let herself stare into the full bucket. There, instantly, was a seeing: a seeing of sudden beauty which took Aggie's breath away with shock. She saw her mother's face, still pale but no longer ghastly with illness, and wearing a smile of peace and contentment. A light shone softly on her face, from a candle lamp set on a silver candlestick; the candlestick was twisted like barley sugar and seemed to Aggie vaguely familiar. Mam had one hand raised to her cheek and the light gleamed on her wedding ring.

Aggie came slowly to her senses, transfixed with happiness. Sam found her when he came to wash his face at the pump, and asked what she was grinning at.

'I saw Mam, Sammy,' said Aggie, coming to herself. 'Mam, in a shining light. It must be Heaven.'

'How did she look?' asked Sam, keenly interested.

'Like she was better, and pleased about things,' said Aggie. 'Smiling. I saw her ring in the light.'

'They'll have had that off her, before they buried her. Goose will have got that ring,' said Sam.

Eliza Goose's screech of 'Aggie! Where's me water?' sent Aggie scurrying into the cottage. Sam followed, hiding behind her, but was still seen and laughed at by Eliza for his tears.

When Dad came in, with some beer aboard, Eliza produced meat and potatoes for him and for herself (the young ones' mouths watered) and related to him all the misdoings of the children. Melia had been whingeing,

Sam had been rude and impertinent, Aggie had been idle and not brought the water in. Dad said nothing while he chewed (food always came before business, with him): and Aggie only half listened to this tirade, glowing secretly with the delight of her vision of Mam.

Finally Dad put down his knife and fork and spat out a piece of gristle.

'Sam, I'm a-warning you,' he said. 'If Miss Goose complains of you again, you'll feel me walking stick good and proper—and that's a promise. Melia, pull yer socks up, gal; you ought to be a help, not a hindrance. As for you, Aggie, if you're no use here you can take yerself off again.'

'What?' said Aggie through her dreams. 'First you turn me out, then you fetch me back. Are you turning me out again, now?'

'That's right,' said Dad. 'I am. Me and Eliza don't want you here, so you can go.'

'Where?' said Aggie, torn between hope for herself and anxiety for Sam and Melia.

'Where you like,' said Dad.

'What about me not bringing you in money?' said Aggie.

'We'll see about that when the harvest comes,' said Dad, with a sly look at Eliza.

'I'll go in the morning, then,' said Aggie. 'I'll go with Bert Syme, if he's going.'

'Suit yerself,' said Dad. 'Only don't wake me and Eliza. You'll get me boot round yer earhole, if you do.'

'I'll get up to bed, then,' said Aggie. 'It's an early start.'

With the bedroom a tangle of things she had put out to pack, and the carpet-bag gaping on the floor, Aggie was joined by Sam and Melia.

'Ag, I'm going with you,' said Sam, all in a rush. 'I won't stay. I can get work, I know I can.'

'And if you think I'm staying with her and Dad, all on me own—then think again. I'm coming too,' said Melia.

TWENTY-FOUR

Aggie considered it a miracle that the three young ones got out of the cottage without waking Eliza or their father. Aggie with the carpet-bag, the other two with their possessions stuffed into pillowcases, crept past the bed where Eliza Goose was snuffling in her sleep and Dad snoring heartily. The stairs creaked abominably, Melia skidded down one step in the dark, and the door at the stair's foot swung to with a sharp click behind them. But no shout came from the double bed.

Downstairs, the three put on the boots they had been carrying, and let themselves out quietly into cool, dewy air.

It was March now, and the mornings lighter. Sam and Melia both became high-spirited when they reached the road, cheered by a sense of escape and by the green now showing through the black earth of the wheatfield and the golden haze on the willows as they began to leaf. Aggie was sunk in anxiety about the younger two. Could Sam really get work—and where? And what could be done about Melia, who was plainly still of school age and in need of parental care?

Although they waited an hour or more in the road, Melia complaining continually that she had hurt her ankle on the stairs, there was no sign of Bert Syme and his cart. In the end they gave him up and waited, hiding in the church, until midday, when they cadged lifts off the driver of the brewer's dray which came to the village every Wednesday. It meant crouching among the barrels, as the driver was not supposed to take passengers; and Aggie paid him sixpence for their fare. He put them down on the edge of Marksey, and they went to Gran's at the best pace they could, either Aggie or Sam supporting the hobbling Melia.

It was a shock to Granny Flack to see them all. Aggie and Sam she would have received without surprise; but Melia, and the luggage, startled her out of an after-dinner sleep.

'What's up?' was all she could say.

'Mam died, Gran,' began Aggie.

'So I heard,' said Gran. 'Miss Marriott heard it in the market; she told me. Your dad never thought to ask me to the funeral, nor nothing. Not that I could have got to it; but it's nice to be asked. And who's this here? I'd thank you for telling me.'

'Don't you know Melia, Gran?' said Sam, amazed.

'It ain't likely I would, is it,' said Gran, 'seeing as I never seen her before.'

Melia said nothing, but stood on one leg to rest her bad foot and turned a blank stare on Gran.

'The thing is, now,' said Aggie, 'a woman's moved in with Dad and we can't stand her. Dad turned me out again and the others wouldn't stop without me there.'

'We've run off,' said Sam.

'If you think I can take all of you in, you can think again!' snapped Gran. Her face was set in a scowl and her eyes glared.

'Can't we stop a night, while we plan things out?' begged Aggie.

'Not three of you can't,' said Gran. 'One can, and you'd better sort out which. And then, only for a night or two.'

'I can go back to the farm, Gran,' said Aggie. 'And maybe the Willetts could find somewhere for Melia, too. Sam had better stay with you.'

'I'm getting a job, Gran,' said Sam with pride. 'I can do anything.'

Gran eyed him sceptically, but said nothing. To Aggie

she said, 'I hope you know how you're getting out to the farm, you and the child.'

'Wednesday, ain't it,' said Aggie. 'Prayer meeting. Willetts will be there; they'll take us back, if they'll have us.'

'Maybe you got your head screwed on after all, Aggie Flack,' said Gran. 'If you want to eat, you'd best plan that too. Get off to the market and get us a loaf and something to go with it.'

Sam, who liked the market, opted to go too, but Melia said her foot hurt and stayed with Gran. Gran dozed off and Melia sat staring round the little house, bored and deflated. She had expected an outpouring of sympathy from Gran—with herself, a pretty waif, at the heart of it. To be seen as something of a nuisance left her lost and bewildered.

Aggie and Sam ran to the market place, clattering over cobblestones and cheerful with a sense of escape and optimism. They bought bread and cheese and dawdled among the stalls.

'Look, Aggie!' said Sam as they lingered by a stall selling cheap jewellery. 'There's a brooch like Mam's.'

'Cor blast it!' said Aggie, stopped in her tracks. 'That is Mam's.'

'Can't be,' said Sam. 'Eliza Goose has got that.'

'I never saw her wear it,' said Aggie. 'Likely enough she'd sell it.'

'The bitch!' said Sam. 'That's marked a shilling, Aggie. Buy it!'

Aggie stood staring at the brooch, sudden tears blurring her sight. The brooch was of yellow metal, moulded to represent two hands, clasping each other. Mam never wore it, and Aggie wondered who had given it to Mam and whether it had been given in love. She hated to see something of her mother's put out for sale; and like Sam, she was convinced that it was her mother's. It was like no other brooch she had ever seen.

'Go on, buy it,' said Sam.

'She didn't wear it,' said Aggie. 'How come you recognized it?'

'It were in her sewing box,' said Sam. 'She used to let me have the box, when I were little, to play with the buttons.'

'Me too,' said Aggie. 'Hold the basket, Sam; I'm buying it.'

Aggie had holes in her pockets and a full purse, so she wore the brooch on her coat.

'Let's go to Brother Ernie's stall,' she said to Sam, sniffing away the last of her tears. 'He helped me find a place. He might help you.'

Brother Ernie and his wife sold confectionery; his large earnest face hovered like a solemn moon above his colourful bottles of bull's-eyes, barley sugar, and aniseed balls. He listened, all sympathy, to Aggie's story and Sam's interruptions.

'Matthews, the bakers, want a boy to train,' he said finally, 'but I fear young Samuel's too young.'

'We'll ask,' said Aggie; but they had no luck at Matthews. The boss was away, having gone out to see a local miller.

'Come tomorrow,' said his wife to Sam. 'He'll see you tomorrow. Can you ride a bicycle?'

Sam went back to Granny Flack's with Aggie, his mind entirely occupied by thoughts of bicycling; he ate his bread and cheese in a dream.

Melia was reluctant to go to the chapel prayer meeting with Aggie. 'It'll be all your friends,' she said to Aggie.

'You'd better come, if you want a lift out to the farm,' said Aggie. 'You ain't set on walking, are you?'

Certainly Aggie got a hearty welcome at the meeting, and whispers of sympathy over her mother's death. People spoke kindly to Melia, but Melia replied mainly by silence. This was Aggie's affair and she didn't want to be involved.

Aggie was cast down when the Willetts didn't appear at the meeting.

'Ain't Brother Joseph coming?' she whispered to Mr Osgood, who was there with his family.

'The little boy is poorly,' said Mr Osgood. 'He won't come tonight.'

Aggie explained her and Melia's predicament, and Mr Osgood readily agreed to take the two girls out to Hope Farm. They had their luggage with them, tucked away in a corner of the meeting-room, and after the evening's proceedings were over they fitted themselves into the Osgoods' trap together with Mrs Osgood, Hester, and Miriam. It was a tight squeeze, and Melia—between the two Osgood girls—forgot her huff and talked happily to Miriam.

In the trap, as the horse picked its way slowly by lantern light, Aggie thought with concentration. This was a bad time to throw Melia on the mercy of the Willetts, if they had a sick child in the house. Was it fair to ask the Osgoods if they could take her in?

Mrs Osgood settled that question herself. 'We'd put you up for a few nights if we could, Melia,' she said, 'but we've no spare bed. My parents are staying with us for a while, and the house is full to bursting.'

So the two Flack girls stood on the Hope Farm doorstep, in the dark, with their luggage at their feet, and Aggie knocked bravely at the door.

TWENTY-FIVE

Aggie had put together a neat speech to make to Mr or Mrs Willett—whichever one opened the door—to plead for the hospitality of Hope Farm for herself and Melia. But when Mrs Ruth opened the door, looking white and worried, Aggie's speech was overpowered. The house was full of the energetic screaming of a seriously upset child.

'Cor blast, Mrs Ruth!' exclaimed Aggie. 'Is that our Albie? What's he got?'

'Mumps,' said Mrs Ruth. 'Can you stay and help me, Aggie? Have you come back?'

'Yes, please, Mrs Ruth,' said Aggie. 'And I've had mumps. This here's me sister Melia, and I come to ask—I mean, can she stay here for a bit?'

'Has she had mumps?' said Mrs Ruth.

Melia said 'Yes' but Aggie said, 'No you ain't, Melia—that was measles. Sam and me got mumps over before you was born.'

'Then she'd better not stay here,' said Mrs Ruth. 'Flora's sure to get it; and the last thing we want in this house is another child to nurse.'

'Osgoods are full,' said Aggie. 'Where else—'; and as her mind's eye ran over the houses in the streets and the lanes nearest to Hope Farm, inspiration struck her.

'I know, Mrs Ruth!' she said. 'Mrs Minster. She likes company and she likes me and I know she'd like Melia.'

'Take Melia round there, then; and come back quick as you can,' urged Mrs Ruth. 'If ever a house needed another pair of hands, it's this one, now!'

Mrs Minster was a near neighbour of the Willetts' who often invited Aggie in for a chat. Energetic knocking brought her to the door of the tiny house, a coat over her nightgown and a candle in her hand.

'Mercy, child!' she exclaimed to Aggie. 'What is it? Is it a fire?'

'Nothing bad, Mrs Minster,' said Aggie soothingly. 'All it is, is—our father's living with another woman now and this here's my sister; she couldn't abide that and she's run off and what I mean is, can she stay with you a day or two because there's mumps at the Willetts'?'

Mrs Minster sorted out this jumbled information, and replied by putting down her candle and clasping Melia in her elbowy arms.

'Poor little motherless thing!' she crooned. 'And her so small and pretty! For sure, that's a hard old world out there; but there's a bed for her here, the lamb, as long as she wants it.'

This was a perfect welcome for Melia, who wound her arms round Mrs Minster and wept on to the good cloth of the coat. Tears of relief and fatigue, Aggie supposed; but Aggie never did know when Melia was acting.

Aggie said goodnight and half ran to Willetts', where Mr Joseph was walking the floor with Albie in his arms while Mrs Ruth rocked Flora. The sight of Aggie stopped Flora's tears altogether and Albie's sobs became less determined.

'Abbie, Abbie!' said Flora—the children's name for Aggie. 'Abbie, sing!'

'Welcome back, Aggie Flack!' said Mr Joseph.

'If you can keep Flora's attention for a bit, I'll go and cook us something,' said Mrs Ruth. Aggie sang to Flora until she fell asleep; and even Albie, tormented by his swollen neck, at last nodded off. Mr Joseph and Aggie exchanged satisfied smiles over the children's sleeping heads.

'Well, that's good,' said Mr Joseph. 'We're all glad you're back. The new little one's due in six weeks and Ruth will be having her hands full. Save your story to tell us over supper; but I'm more sorry than I can say about your mother. She is with God, you know.'

'I know,' said Aggie. 'I saw her. It were Heaven, I think; all shining, and she were smiling.'

Mr Joseph gave her a sharp look, but said nothing except that they had better eat supper while peace lasted.

Mrs Ruth had fried them all sausages for supper, and Aggie told all her news while they ate them. 'And oh, Mr Joseph, Mrs Ruth!' she finished up. 'Sam thinks Mam didn't die natural, and I'm frit he may be right.'

'Don't talk about your suspicions to anyone but us, Aggie,' said Mr Joseph. 'Keep a still tongue in your head and use your eyes and ears instead. Certainly, your father and his Miss Goose are doing what they shouldn't, and you and the younger ones are best out of it, especially little Melia.'

'I hope she can stay on at Mrs Minster's,' said Aggie. 'Melia and me are best kept separate; she don't like me and she says she don't want no witch-sister.'

'Dear me!' said Mrs Ruth. 'It sounds as though you're right and the two of you should be in different houses, though when things are easier here we could take Melia in if that seems best.'

'And I'd have holly in me bed again, or groundsel,' moaned Aggie. 'I know you'll say that's heathen superstition, Mr Joseph, but it ain't my superstition, it's Melia's.'

'We'll see when things calm down,' said Mr Joseph.

It was a long time before things calmed down. Before Albie had really begun to recover, Flora got mumps; and not only Flora—Mrs Ruth got it too, having never had it as a child. Hardly were all three invalids on the mend before the new baby arrived, early and with some difficulty. Aggie found herself called upon to act as the midwife's helper, then the doctor's; was praised as a handy girl; and finally saw everybody's effort crowned with the birth of a tiny, delicate, perfect baby girl.

'It's a miracle they're both all right,' said Mr Joseph, holding the baby and smiling foolishly at it. 'We'll call her Grace. That's what we'll call her.'

Mrs Ruth was very feeble for some weeks, and it was not until well into May that Aggie was out and about in the village, with Grace in the pram. She found a changed world.

TWENTY-SIX

By the time Aggie went further afield than the Hope Farm farmyard and garden, Mrs Ruth was beginning to pick up strength and get back some of her natural pale peach colour, and the twins were back to their normal buoyancy; Grace was putting on weight and smiling. Aggie had entirely lost her heart to Grace, feeling that Grace's safety was in part her own achievement. Every sign of the baby's flourishing was a joy to her and every wail a misery.

'Can I take her out, Mrs Ruth?' she asked one bright day. 'Can I take her to show Melia and Mrs Minster?'

'Yes, of course,' said Mrs Ruth; so Aggie crammed on her coat and hat and stowed Grace, well-shawled, safely in the pram. She escaped without being seen by Albie and Flora, who would have wanted to come too.

It was Saturday, so Melia would not be at school. Melia now attended the village school, with the Osgoods, and seemed to be successful and happy there; she also went to the parish church, as Mrs Minster was 'church'. Aggie had caught glimpses from the Hope Farm windows of Melia on the way to school, hand-in-hand with Miriam Osgood, and of Melia walking tidily beside Mrs Minster looking like everyone's model of a good child. She had, Aggie noticed, a new coat and a pretty blue umbrella.

With great care Aggie manoeuvred the pram to Mrs Minster's. She saw movement inside the house, as she looked in at the window; but nobody answered her knock. She knocked again, and again got no answer.

It occurred to her that Mrs Minster might be too busy to come to the door, and Melia might be at Osgoods'. So to Osgoods' she went. Hester answered the door, turned bright red and began to shut it again.

'Hester!' said Aggie urgently. 'Can't I see you? Don't you want to look at the baby?'

'Mother says we've not to talk to you,' said Hester.

'Why not?' demanded Aggie, baffled.

'You know, Aggie,' half whispered Hester.

'Danged if I do,' said Aggie. 'Say out what you mean, Hester Osgood.'

'I don't like to,' said Hester. 'But it's what Melia says.'

'What does she say?' Aggie asked, angry now.

'That you're a witch,' said Hester under her breath.

'It's not true, Hester, it's not true!' cried Aggie—feeling her cheeks flush and her stomach clench as her world turned over.

'I can't see you, Aggie. Mother says,' said Hester, and the door closed.

Aggie went on up the village street, watching carefully how people reacted to her. Some faces turned away. A few people crossed the street to avoid her. Others stopped to look under the hood of the pram at Grace asleep, but their eyes wouldn't meet Aggie's eyes. Aggie went home in despair. She told Mrs Ruth she was back, settled Grace in her cot, went up to her own room, and flung herself on her bed (still in her coat and boots) and cried as she had seldom cried before.

After a time Mrs Ruth, puzzled by her absence, called her at the bottom of the attic stairs; and getting no reply, toiled up them. Seeing Aggie's desolate state she knelt down beside her, took one of Aggie's clenched fists in one of her hands and stroked Aggie's rough hair.

'What is it, Aggie? Tell me,' she said. 'It can't be Grace—she's all right. So what's happened? It will be better if you tell.'

Aggie could hardly get the words out. 'They say . . .

they say I'm a witch,' she gasped. 'It's what Melia said. Mrs Minster wouldn't . . . wouldn't open her door; Hester said . . . she said their mother wouldn't let them talk to me. People dodged me in the street. Oh, Mrs Ruth, what am I to do?'

'Oh, mercy!' said Mrs Ruth, and sighed. 'I should have thought of this when I said you could go out.'

'You mean you knew?' said Aggie. She lifted her dishevelled head and stared at Mrs Ruth. 'You knew? Mr Joseph knew? And you never turned me out?'

'Of course not, Aggie,' said Mrs Ruth. 'You had already told us about your odd gift—'

'Ain't no gift!' Aggie interrupted.

'And what's more, we know your character,' said Mrs Ruth. 'We know you are honest, and we know you are kind. I'm afraid we don't know the same of Melia.'

'Who told you? About witchcraft? Was it Melia did?' asked Aggie.

'The vicar felt it was his duty to warn Joseph that his housemaid had an evil reputation,' said Mrs Ruth, and suddenly giggled. 'Joseph sent him off with a flea in his ear—gave him a sermon on Christian charity! Poor vicar!'

'Huh!' said Aggie.

'Now, Aggie, we've got to keep our heads about this,' said Mrs Ruth. 'Joseph and I know that you yourself are innocent; but we don't know that an evil power is not using you. You might be possessed.'

'Possessed!' exclaimed Aggie, horrified. 'You mean by the devil? That I'm in the devil's power and he's using me and I'll go to hell? Where there's burning for ever and gnashing of teeth? If Mr Joseph believes that then he surely will turn me out, and where shall I go?'

'Calm yourself, child,' said Mrs Ruth. 'Sit up, and take this hanky, and we'll say a prayer.'

Mrs Ruth's prayer was all about the innocent being

proved innocent, the guilty proved guilty and the guilty forgiven. Aggie said Amen to this but it did strike her uncomfortably that she was being asked to forgive Melia. She supposed she would have to try, though she would much rather have brooded on Melia's spitefulness and her own wronged innocence.

Joseph Willett, when he came home, agreed that Aggie was free of blame but possibly in danger. 'The next thing to do,' he said cheerfully, 'is to talk about all this in chapel.'

The idea of having her reputation made a public matter in the chapel shocked Aggie. 'Oh, no, please, Mr Joseph,' she said. 'I don't want any more talk about it. That upsets me so.'

'You'll find there's already talk about it at chapel,' said Mr Joseph. 'What one person in a small community knows, they all know. If the Osgoods shy away from you in the village, they'll do the same in chapel.'

'These things are better faced,' agreed Mrs Ruth. 'I don't think tomorrow, do you, Joseph? At the prayer meeting on Wednesday would be best.'

'Quite so,' said Mr Joseph. 'Tomorrow, Aggie, you stay at home with the children and give Ruth a chance to come to chapel. Then on Wednesday you and I will go.'

'Mr Joseph, how can I face it?' Aggie sighed. 'And are you sure you trust the children to me?'

Mr Joseph said, 'God will be with you,' and Mrs Ruth said, 'Yes, we trust you; and the children do, too.'

'Then if that's all settled, I'd better get some work done,' said Aggie valiantly. Mrs Ruth patted her shoulder and Aggie took a mop and bucket and tackled the brick floor of the kitchen.

The day had one more shock in store for her. She was so troubled by her fears that she failed to shut her eyes when she dusted the tall mirror in the hall. And suddenly it was there again: the bright hillside, the dark wood. But she was nearer now to the wood, further down the steep side of the hill. She could see into the woodland, between the trees; and she saw movement there, something darker than the trees: a figure, human perhaps, but if so crouching like an animal, moving with stealth.

The sight dissolved as Aggie screamed out 'No!' Mr Joseph had gone out to the fields; Mrs Ruth was upstairs feeding Grace. Only the twins heard and came running to investigate Aggie's cry. They were convinced that Aggie had seen a mouse and Albie went to fetch the cat while Flora searched the hallway.

By dinnertime the twins had forgotten the mouse and Aggie had mastered her horror. The mastery was only temporary, and from time to time she would remember the vision and the same fear would return. When it did, she shook and sweated and gritted her teeth to stop them from chattering. She even resorted to her old comfort of rhyme and muttered to herself at intervals:

'I'm Aggie Flack
And I won't be frit
Nor I won't turn back
Nor I ain't no witch!
That tell-tale-tit
Is a cat and a bitch.'
('Nor I can't forgive her,' she added to herself.)

The afternoon brought a cheering surprise in a visit from Sam, who was now a bicycle-rider and had ridden over from Marksey to show off his progress and the beauty of his machine.

While things had been getting more stormy for Aggie, they had been settling into place for Sam. Matthews the bakers had in the end taken him on as delivery-boy; and for what he earned from Matthews, Brother Ernie and Sister Flo gave him a bed and his meals. Their own son had recently left home to go overseas, and Sam—lucky Sam—had stepped into the gap. 'Nice to have a lad about again,' his landlord and landlady said contentedly. Sam understood their kindness and responded with cheerful affection.

With Mrs Ruth's permission, Aggie escorted him off to the rickyard and in that quiet place told him about her present difficulties.

'Cor blast, Aggie!' said Sam after hearing it all. 'What's got into Melia, to be such a cat?'

'She don't like me, and never has,' said Aggie sadly. 'But what'll I do about this chapel business?'

'Let the Willetts handle it,' advised Sam. 'They know what's what in that chapel, and they're on your side.'

'All right, then, Sam,' said Aggie. 'You aren't half a help. Next time you come over, ask if you can stay Saturday night. There's a little old camp bed up in that attic; and I'm sure Mrs Ruth wouldn't grudge you a tea.'

All the same, it was a very grey-faced and nervous Aggie who climbed into the trap with Mr Joseph on Wednesday evening.

'Sniff the air, Aggie!' said Mr Joseph encouragingly.

'Ah, I smell the may blossom,' said Aggie. 'That whiffs lovely.'

'And hear the birds, and forget your worries,' said Mr Joseph. 'God is good.'

'Ah,' said Aggie; but a thought something like 'handsome is as handsome does' ran through her mind.

As they went into the prayer meeting, heads turned to look at Aggie, and a momentary hush fell. Nobody smiled. They all know, thought Aggie. Mr Joseph held her firmly by the arm and steered her to a seat near the front.

The beginning of the meeting was a jumble to Aggie, but her wandering mind came abruptly to attention when Mr Joseph stood up to pray.

'O Lord!' said Mr Joseph. 'We are troubled and vexed in our minds about one of the young ones of our number, and we ask for guidance. This young sister stands accused of sorcery, Lord: a deadly sin which can lead to damnation and the flames of hell.'

'Ah!' breathed most of the people there.

'But, Lord,' continued Mr Joseph, 'we know we are not set as judges over each other's souls, only as guardians and guides; and we know we ought not to judge this child of thine. We seek wisdom: we seek counsel: we ask to be shown the right from the wrong. Lead us in thy righteousness and make thy way plain before our faces.'

Mr Joseph sat down and there was a profound silence. Until Aggie stood up, knowing with certainty what to say.

'Lord God, show the truth and show it good and clear!' she said. 'Show as the innocent is innocent and save them from the flames of hell, and show who's guilty and let them be the ones as suffer. You know me, Lord, and that I never meant no harm nor done no harm; so please lift me out of the horrible pit and out of the miry clay, and though I'm not patient like Job and I ain't got boils get me out of trouble like you did him and don't let the devil and his lies come out on top.'

The Biblical language and references of this prayer must have made some impression: many people said 'Amen' and Aggie sat down relieved and even hopeful.

There were a few more prayers about being saved from hell; and finally Brother Ernie stood up.

'This here ain't a prayer, brothers and sisters,' he said. 'It's a thought I've had and perhaps it's heavenly guidance. What we need in this here matter, that's a wise counsellor. We ain't got a minister of our own to be a wise counsellor, but we know of one not far off. Reverend Baldry, now, brethren. He don't live too far off and Brother Joseph and young Aggie, they could visit him. He's infirm in his legs, brethren, but he's wise in his head.'

The meeting prayed over this suggestion and settled that Brother Ernie's idea was the result of divine guidance. Brother Ernie, Brother Joseph, and Aggie were all to go to visit the old, retired minister for a judgement in Aggie's case.

Aggie heard the decision with a mixture of hope and apprehension.

TWENTY-SEVEN

The Reverend Mr Baldry lived outside the Fens: because of his rheumatism, he had moved to a drier, higher area. Brothers Ernie and Joseph settled between them that the best way to get to Mr Baldry's was by train. Aggie was wild with excitement at the thought of a train journey, and Sam when he heard about it was wild with envy. None of the Flack children had ever been on a train.

But when the day for the journey came, anxiety was stronger in Aggie than any pleasurable looking forward. If Mr Baldry gave his judgement against her, the chapel people would ban her and Hope Farm would turn her out: even the trustful Willetts could not harbour a practiser of divination.

The day began badly, with Mr Joseph's cob, which pulled the trap, found to be lame. In the end Mr Osgood, who knew the errand they were on, drove Joseph and Aggie to the station in Marksey—but they would have to find their own way back, as Mr Osgood's business would be finished by midday (it was Saturday) and his family expecting him home.

The next disaster was that Brother Ernie had not arrived at the station when the train came in. Mr Joseph was anxiously pacing up and down; Aggie was stiff as a block, rigid with an assortment of fears. The massive engine was hissing steam like a threshing machine—and no Ernie.

'Oh, what'll we do, Mr Joseph? What'll we do?' wailed Aggie, finding her paralysed tongue as the train whistled.

'Get on,' said Mr Joseph with sudden decision. He

dragged a door open, flung Aggie inside and leapt after her as the train began to move.

'But Brother Ernie—' said Aggie as she subsided into a seat. The carriage was empty except for the two of them.

'I don't suppose he's forgotten, and God forbid he's ill,' said Mr Joseph. 'Either he's made a mistake and gone by an earlier train, or he's delayed—in which case he'll come on later. But Mr Baldry's expecting us at his house at two o'clock, and God willing, that's where we'll be.'

'Oh, mercy!' said Aggie, struck by a new horror. 'The basket with our sandwiches—I've been and gone and left it on the station!'

'Are you sure?' said Mr Joseph, looking put out. Then he started to laugh, and in the end Aggie laughed too.

'Hunger won't hurt us, Aggie,' he said; 'and it's just as well, as hungry we shall be. I can feed my mind, at any rate.' He dived into the pocket of his black coat and Aggie for a moment hoped that he had a secret supply of food there. But what he brought out was his Bible, and he solemnly read while Aggie watched the flying countryside. Fen—fen—more fen; and at last some landscape with a gentle roll to it and soil made grey-brown by the chalk in it.

'That ain't proper ground, is it?' asked Aggie, drawing Mr Joseph's attention to a newly dug patch. 'That's all pale and wishy-washy.'

'Good earth, all the same,' said Mr Joseph. 'Different soil's good for different things. This area grows corn—wheat and barley.'

Aggie forgot her worries in the interest of new places—land, towns, and villages; but they came back with a rush when the train stopped and Mr Joseph got to his feet.

'We aren't getting out here, are we?' she demanded. 'This here ain't a proper station!'

'It's a halt,' said Mr Joseph. 'Only a few trains stop here. But it's the place we want.'

Aggie was still bewildered when they were out of the train and looking around. There were farm buildings not far off, but no town and only a few houses.

'Where does he live?' she asked nervously.

'We've a walk ahead of us,' said Mr Joseph. 'About a mile and a half. It won't take us long, and we're blessed with a fine day.'

'I wish we were blessed with our dinner!' said Aggie. 'Why don't we ask at the farm, Mr Joseph? They'd surely give us a bite of something—even if it's only bread and water.'

The farm produced something better than bread and water. It produced a talkative farmer's wife, whose chattering, Aggie thought, was hiding an illness or a fear, and it produced glasses of milk and slices of seed cake. Aggie and Mr Joseph went smartly on their way, well satisfied; and the farmer's wife pocketed sixpence and nodded them goodbye. She shouted after them something which Mr Joseph did not hear and Aggie did not understand: it sounded like 'Keep to the road!'

The sun shone on them and the road was thick with dried out mud. Their well-polished boots were soon covered by dust and it muffled their steps. They didn't talk as they walked, both intent on their thoughts. Aggie tried to make a walking song, but her anxiety was not the sort which turns to verse; she listened to the singing birds with ears sharpened by a steadily growing sense of panic.

Cor blast, Aggie Flack, she thought to herself. Anyone'd say you was going to your death, girl, not just to see an old man with rheumatics. 'Death, death, death,' her footsteps echoed on the road.

'What do you say we go the footpath way?' said Mr Joseph, interrupting her thoughts. He stopped suddenly at a stile in the hedgerow, and Aggie cannoned into him before she could co-ordinate mind and feet.

'Through fields, is it?' she asked. 'I'd like that better than this old road.'

'It's a bit longer, but we've time in hand,' said Mr Joseph.

He pulled out his pocket watch, opened the hinged disc which covered the dial, and checked. 'Yes,' he said. 'We can just do it, and this way is a pleasant walk.'

'How come you know about it?' asked Aggie as she climbed the stile.

'I've been to see Mr Baldry before; and he told me about this pathway,' said Mr Joseph.

'The grass will dust our boots,' said Aggie. She scuffled through the tufts of the grassy footpath and enjoyed the springiness of the turf. The path took them through pastureland with grazing cattle and buttercups, then gently down and up again between the young green of cornfields. Then there was pasture again; the brow of a small hill; and Aggie stopped in her tracks, choking on a scream.

'No, Mr Joseph, no!' she half sobbed, struggling with the words, almost overpowered with horror.

'What do you mean—"No"?' demanded Mr Joseph.

'No—we can't go down there; we mustn't,' said Aggie. Below them lay a steep slope down, then a tangle of dark-green woodland—all too familiar to Aggie. 'I've seen it,' she brought out. 'I've seen it three times, and I know. There's something in the wood.'

TWENTY-EIGHT

'Something, Aggie? What sort of something?' Mr Joseph
asked. 'God is our protector; we should not be scared of
shadows.'

'Like a man, but it crouches,' said Aggie. 'Oh please,
Mr Joseph! Don't go.'

Mr Joseph did not give way immediately. He coaxed
Aggie, he was firm with Aggie; he was even sharp with
Aggie. Aggie remained gripped by a fear she could
neither describe nor understand, and shuddered from
head to foot with the strength of it.

At last Mr Joseph gave in.

'I can see we'd best not go that way, with you in such
a state,' he said to Aggie. 'Calm yourself, now, and we'll
say a prayer.'

He took off his black hat and clasped it to his chest.
Aggie heard not a single word of the prayer until it got
to 'Amen'; and her eyes never left the wood. She still
shook in spasms and her teeth chattered.

'Come along,' said Mr Joseph, not unkindly. He took
her arm, turned her round, and towed her with him as
they retraced their steps towards the road.

'Look lively, Aggie,' he said. 'We've lost a quarter of
an hour, or more, by our detour; that'll be half an hour
when we get back to the road. We'll be late at Mr
Baldry's.'

'I'm sorry,' said Aggie. 'But I couldn't have gone
down there. I couldn't. Nor you shouldn't, neither; you
was in danger too.'

'Don't think about it,' said Mr Joseph. 'Think about
the flowers. What's that one, the little yellow and orange
thing?'

'Hens-and-chickens. You know it,' said Aggie, allowing herself to be distracted.

'Bird's-foot trefoil is its proper name,' said Mr Joseph. 'Now you ask me one.'

They botanized their way back to the road, and walked on briskly in their original direction, branching off after a while into a network of lanes and by-roads. After they had left the main road they heard the noise of a gang of people on it, and looking back, saw the distant shapes of a crowd, some in a cart, some on bicycles, and some on foot, apparently carrying sticks, clubs, and even guns.

'Nothing to do with us,' said Mr Joseph, turning away. 'Don't loiter, Aggie. We're already late. But you look better, and I hope you feel it.'

'I do, but I'm blasted hot,' sighed Aggie. At least her sticky discomfort was a counter to her two panics—over divination, and over the shape in the wood—and she arrived at Mr Baldry's flustered mainly by dirt, dust, and sweat.

Mr Baldry came to his cottage door himself, opening a small dark door in a bower of honeysuckle. He surprised Aggie by being tiny, almost a dwarf, and having a clean-shaven face almost as brown and creased as an autumn leaf. In it, his eyes looked pale and filmy; and Aggie noticed a white stick propped near the door. Mr Baldry was blind.

'You'll take a bite after your journey?' he said, and pottered skilfully about the dark room of his cottage fetching ginger beer and seed cake. Mr Joseph and Aggie grinned over their slices of cake.

Mr Baldry's questions to Aggie were quiet and careful. He wanted to know about all the seeings she could remember, and about which of them had been followed by events linked to them. Aggie reckoned that they had all been prophetic to some degree, except the vision of her mother in Heaven.

'I've seen lamps like the one you describe,' said Mr Baldry. 'A travelling pedlar brought them, door to door, some years ago before my sight went.'

'But she must have been in Heaven, Mr Baldry,' insisted Aggie. 'She were dead at the time I saw her; and it were all light where she were.'

Most interesting of all to Mr Baldry was Aggie's description of the three seeings of the hillside and the wood. 'Sharp's Wood,' he said as she described it. When she had been through the whole story twice, Mr Baldry suggested she went into his garden and took a rest.

'And look in the pool,' he added slyly.

Aggie wandered the small neat garden, which had two apple trees, beds of lavender and pinks, and a shadowy narrow pool. She saw nothing in this but her reflection and a few fat red carp, who rose up gaping to be fed.

They're talking about me inside, Aggie thought restlessly. Mr Baldry's asking Mr Joseph about me character and whether I make things up and tell lies . . .

Irresistibly tempted, she crept close to the open window.

' . . . a genuine, good-hearted girl and willing to learn what the chapel has to teach,' Mr Joseph was saying. 'Her sister, now—that's a different tale entirely.'

Aggie pulled quickly away from the window. It was like shade in fierce heat to hear kind things said about herself; but she preferred not to hear what was said about Melia.

The reference to the chapel put it into her head that she should say a prayer for a fair judgement from Mr Baldry, and she sat on a bench under an apple tree putting her thoughts into order. Distant shots distracted her: people after rabbits, she supposed.

She was even more distracted by the arrival of Brother Ernie, unsafely mounted on a wobbling, rattling lady's bicycle. He puffed to a halt at Mr Baldry's gate, and Aggie went to open it for him.

'Missed the train,' gasped Ernie. 'Got the next. Found this old bike leaning on a gate and I thought, God provides. I'll put it back later.'

'They're indoors, Mr Shutter,' said Aggie. 'Mr Baldry's got ginger beer and seed cake.'

Ernie sighed loudly, tapped on the little door, and let himself in.

Aggie grew well and truly tired of sitting in the garden. She thought the whole story must have been rehearsed again for Ernie's benefit, it all took so long. She was just, for the fifth time, counting the carp in the pool, when a trap drew up to Mr Baldry's door and a broad-shouldered, brown-skinned man in shirtsleeves, whom Aggie immediately labelled 'farmer', got out and was let into the cottage.

Cor blast, thought Aggie, Mr Baldry don't have a quiet life. Let's hope he don't want one.

To her surprise, she was not called into the cottage again to hear a verdict on her case. Mr Baldry came out, alone, and called her to sit by him on the bench under the apple tree.

'Well, Aggie,' he said. 'Did you see any visions in my pool?'

'Nothing but fish,' said Aggie. 'I tried to count, but I couldn't see them all at once.'

'That's good,' said Mr Baldry.

'Why?' demanded Aggie.

'If you were a storyteller, only wanting to attract attention to yourself, you'd have made certain you saw something in that pool,' said Mr Baldry, and laughed. 'To be serious, Aggie, I see no complications in this matter of yours,' he went on in his quiet way. 'It seems to me that you are not practising any witchcraft, but that you are being used by God as a channel for warnings. In which case, we should praise God for his mercies. You must speak freely about what you see and perhaps lives can be saved by that; but you should never seek out visions—that way, false seeings may come.'

'Warnings . . . ' said Aggie, made thoughtful by his grave manner. 'You mean, Bowleses' baby? But if I'd told Bowleses, the baby would have drowned all the same. It would be bound to; I'd seen it.'

'As to that, I can't say,' said Mr Baldry. 'Maybe so. But I am also thinking of today. The caller who just came brought bad news, and I am needed to go and sit with the dead and the bereaved.'

'The shooting?' whispered Aggie.

'You refused to go into Sharp's Wood today, or to let our dear Joseph go,' said Mr Baldry. 'Half an hour ago, two men died in that wood.'

TWENTY-NINE

'What happened?' asked Aggie, beginning to shake again at the memory of her fear.

'A man was hiding out in the wood,' said Mr Baldry; 'a poor soul, who had killed another man in a fight and then run mad with the dread and the shame of what he had done. He went out last night and stole a shotgun from a farm. The men off two farms, and the local constable, went today to take him; but as I say, this was a madman. He shot a young farmer, who has died; and then shot himself. A tragic business.'

'It could have been us,' muttered Aggie.

'Likely so,' said Mr Baldry. 'I have to leave now, to take consolation and prayers. A trap has come to fetch me, and the man would be willing to take you three to the railway. Are you ready to go?'

'Yes, and thank you,' said Aggie. As they both got to their feet she gave Mr Baldry, who was little taller than she was, an impulsive hug which nearly toppled him over.

'You're proper kind,' said Aggie. 'You're not a bit like I thought you would be—all doom and whiskers; and I'm so glad, so glad, you don't think I'm going to hell for a witch.'

'Give me your arm to the house,' said Mr Baldry. 'Not a witch, Aggie, but a bit of a prophet. Heed your warnings.'

Brother Ernie and Mr Joseph both shook Aggie warmly by the hand, and a cheerful party started back homewards, bicycle and all. Aggie slept most of the way in the train, overcome by relief and heat.

Mr Joseph waked her when they reached Marksey,

and while he went ahead to hire a cab to take him and Aggie to Hope Farm, and Brother Ernie said goodbye, Aggie retrieved Mrs Ruth's basket from under a station seat.

As the cab clopped slowly back to Hardingley, Aggie and Mr Joseph ate their cold mutton sandwiches.

Aggie took a swig from a bottle of cold tea and asked, licking her lips, 'What am I going to say to Melia?'

'As little as possible,' said Mr Joseph. 'I shall want to talk to young Melia, myself.'

It was several days before Aggie saw Melia—happy days of relief, and of being rejoiced over by Mrs Ruth and apologetically approached by the Osgoods.

'I'm real sorry,' said Hester, stopping Aggie, and Grace's pram, in the street. Hester turned almost beetroot-red and tears came into her eyes. 'Mother's sorry too, and Miriam. It was all a mistake, what we thought; Mr Willett told my father so.'

Miriam ran up at this point and added her 'Sorry' to Hester's.

'It weren't your fault,' said Aggie. 'You was told lies. Mr Joseph says I must go to chapel, Sunday, so everyone can see I'm not a sinner, and he'll tell out what Mr Baldry said.'

'You saved his life—Joseph Willett's,' said Miriam in a low voice.

'I had a warning from God,' said Aggie piously, and went triumphantly on her way.

It was the next day, another Saturday, that she saw Melia, coming down the lane as if she had just come away from Hope Farm.

'You bitch, Aggie Flack!' shouted Melia across the road.

'Bitch what for?' Aggie called back.

'What you told Mr Willett!' said Melia, anger grating in her voice and glinting in her eyes.

'I never told him. Vicar told him,' said Aggie, and turned away. She found she was trembling, her own rage answering Melia's. 'If you've found out what you are, who's to blame?' she called over her shoulder.

'Cor blast,' she muttered to herself, back in Hope Farm. 'I'm supposed to forgive her. Some hopes . . .'

'Have you seen your sister?' asked Mr Joseph as Aggie was serving up the potatoes for dinner.

'Yes. I didn't say nothing, but she shouted out at me,' said Aggie. 'What did you say to her?'

'That's between her and me. But I warned her of the mischief a spiteful tongue can do,' said Mr Joseph. Aggie tried not to smile, but was sure her satisfaction showed.

On Sunday, the satisfaction grew as the chapel people acknowledged her with smiles and nods. (Not all: some eyes avoided her and Aggie well knew it would take time before 'No smoke without fire' stopped being said.) This was her first return to chapel: the previous Sunday, Mr Joseph had advised that she should stay home until the news of her rehabilitation by Mr Baldry could be given to the Wednesday meeting, and discussed there.

Aggie was pleased to be smiled at, to feel again that she belonged here; she was also pleased to find Sam in the congregation. Sam made his way up to her after the service, grinning.

'So you ain't a witch, our Aggie,' he said. 'I'd like to have heard what you said to Melia!'

'I don't talk to Melia, Sam,' said Aggie. 'She miscalled me in the street, but I never started it. Nor I won't.'

'I got some news,' said Sam. 'Gran heard it from a neighbour that heard it from Bert Syme in the market. Eliza Goose have left our dad.'

Aggie was brought up short by this news. 'For sure, Sam?' she asked. 'What for?'

'Gran said, he started to knock her about when he was sozzled—like he used to with us,' Sam answered. 'She went back to her old mam and that poor daft Luke.'

'Reckon they need her more than Dad does,' said Aggie. 'But what'll Dad do now?'

'Find some other darned fool woman to look after him, I should think,' said Sam.

All the way back to Hope Farm Aggie thought about Sam's news, with vague foreboding. But she told herself that Sam was right—Dad would find some other woman.

It was a horrible shock for her, when the trap drew up at the farm gates, to see her father lounging against the wall.

THIRTY

'Oh no!' she gasped out, clutching at Mr Joseph's sleeve. 'Cor blast, Mr Joseph! It's me dad.'

'So I see,' said Mr Joseph. 'I'll come back to speak to him when I've put the trap away. Don't agree to anything, Aggie.'

'Goodnight!' Aggie groaned. She jumped down to open the gates, and after she had closed them behind the trap went up to her father. 'Well, Dad!' she said.

'Well, is it?' grunted Dad. 'What's well about it? I'm a poor widow-man, left on his own, and his children skipped off and deserted him.'

'I never skipped off,' said Aggie. 'I were turned out, as you should remember. And if the others skipped off—like as not that had something to do with being half starved.'

'So you blame me for being poor,' said Dad.

'No, I don't. I blame you for being stingy,' said Aggie. Her hands were driven well down into her pockets and she stood heavily planted, feet well apart, to fight her corner.

'That weren't my fault—it were that Lizzie Goose,' Dad protested. 'She never could make the money go round.'

'There never were much money, as I remember,' said Aggie.

'As to that,' said Dad, straightening himself up; 'how's the harvest coming along, Aggie Flack?'

'Middling good,' said Aggie reluctantly. She hated the thought of Joseph, Ruth, and the farmhands' hard work making money for Dad to spend at the Nag's Head; but she supposed he might have some legal right over her earnings.

'Good day, Mr Flack,' said Mr Joseph, coming briskly out of the yard gates. 'You've come to enquire after your daughter's health, I take it?'

'Something more than that,' said Dad, and grinned. 'The fact is, I'm feeling the need of a gal at home.'

Mr Joseph frowned, and Aggie grew deep red with distress and dismay.

'Your daughter is a regular chapelgoer, Mr Flack,' Mr Joseph said. 'And she's young and should be protected from all kinds of moral danger. I would feel most unhappy at her going into a house where her father lived with a concubine.'

Good shot, Mr Joseph, thought Aggie. That'll never work, though; more's the pity.

'You've been hearing gossip, Mr Willett,' said Dad, shaking his head till his cap bounced. 'That's terrible, what chattering tongues can say. It's true I had a housekeeper for a while, but she ain't with me no more—she left. That's how it is I need a gal at home.'

'Have you heard about this, Aggie?' Mr Joseph asked; and Aggie had reluctantly to admit that Sam had given her an account of Dad's being left on his own.

'This is hardly good for Aggie, Mr Flack!' said Mr Joseph, standing his tallest (a head and a half above Dad) and looking his most severe. 'Twice she's been thrown out of her home by you, and now you come wanting her back. She needs some stability in her life; she needs to know where she is. She's doing well here, and my wife needs her. You can't just—'

'Give over!' shouted Dad. 'Did I say I wanted her? No, I didn't. Great daft lummox of a thing! Her and me never did agree. It's the little pretty one I come for, and I'll thank you to tell me where she is.'

'Melia! You want Melia?' asked Mr Joseph, considerably startled. 'Surely she's only eight—'

'Nine,' put in Aggie, momentarily sorry that she had not marked Melia's birthday.

'Too young to act as your housekeeper,' finished Mr Joseph.

'Who said housekeeper?' demanded Dad. 'She'll go to school, like she ought. Evenings, she can cook my bit of supper and run a broom round the room. Plenty of nine year olds do that for a widow-man.'

'He'll overwork her, Mr Joseph,' pleaded Aggie. She knew that Dad's taking Melia home to run the cottage would doom Melia to receiving all the hard knocks Mam had taken. Mam had stood it; but what it would do to a child like Melia was a horrifying thought.

'Take me instead, Dad,' she said, forcing the words from a resisting tongue. 'I'm better able than she is. We can get on if we try.'

'You heard me,' said Dad, bunching his fists. 'I'm taking Melia. She's in the farmhouse, is she?'

'No, she ain't!' cried Aggie, with some hope of fighting a rearguard action.

'Go gently, Aggie,' said Mr Joseph, putting a hand on her shoulder. 'Your father does have a right to take your sister, just as he did to take you. Equally, you have a right to make sure she's well treated. Maybe you and Sam could go over in a week or two—'

'I won't have them in the house,' said Dad. 'They skipped, and that's that. Does somebody tell me where my daughter is, or do I ask the police?'

'The cottage with white shutters, down the lane,' said Mr Willett. 'But have a care, Mr Flack. Eyes will be on you.'

'You on about God again?' said Dad, and spat towards the gutter.

'I hope you're not proposing to make the child walk to Little Needham,' said Mr Joseph.

'I ain't,' said Dad. 'I got a trap.'

'That's Doctor Mortlock's!' exclaimed Aggie, following his pointing finger. A sagging horse and a ramshackle trap were visible further up the street, where the village horse-trough stood.

'Borrowed it,' said Dad. 'I'll be on me way.'

Mr Joseph went into the house, but Aggie stood in the street, struggling with tears. She half expected to hear screams from Mrs Minster's, but when after about twenty minutes Dad and Melia came out of the cottage they were both silent. Mrs Minster stood on the doorstep, weeping copiously. Melia, carrying her belongings (a larger bundle than she had arrived with), went, white-faced and tearless, towards the doctor's trap.

'I hate you, Aggie Flack!' she hissed as she passed. 'You told him where I was. Witch, witch!'

'It weren't me,' said Aggie. 'Melia, I'm sorry; Melia, write to me!'

'She won't have time for that,' said Dad, with a triumphant grin.

Aggie stood to watch the trap drive off, but neither Melia nor Dad looked towards her. She went back into the house dissolved in tears, and was very little use to Mrs Ruth for the remainder of the day.

'It's nearly school holiday time,' said Mrs Ruth. 'It won't be too hard for Melia, at first.'

'She'll want to be off playing with her friends, not working in the house,' sniffed Aggie. 'There'll be trouble between her and Dad. And I don't like what Dad said—he said, "I want the little pretty one." I don't like it, Mrs Ruth.'

'I understand,' said Mrs Ruth. 'But don't give up hope, Aggie. Joseph may be able to think of something to do.'

Aggie would hardly have been cheered if she had known how Mr Joseph's 'doing something' would turn out.

THIRTY-ONE

Aggie spent the next few weeks in a torment of anxiety about Melia.

Sam was no great comfort. He came to spend Saturday night the weekend after Melia left; Mrs Ruth put an old straw mattress on the folding bed for him, in the empty part of the attic beyond Aggie's room. He needed only a pillow, and a sheet to go over him: it was a heavy, stuffy spell of weather, with frequent thunder showers. With Aggie's bedroom door open, the two could talk as they lay in their beds.

'Mam said, "Don't let the little ones fret"—like as if I ought to look after you two,' said Aggie. 'And I ain't looked after Melia, Sam.'

'What Dad done ain't your fault,' insisted Sam. 'You couldn't have stopped him. And don't try it on, looking after me, Aggie Flack; I'm all right.'

'I know that,' said Aggie. 'It's one thing I'm thankful for. But I worry night and day about Melia.'

'It won't get you nowhere,' said Sam. 'She wouldn't worry about you.'

In the end Aggie wrote a letter to Melia, and another to Carrie Bean. The one to Melia said,

> *Dear Mely, I'm proper sorry Dad took you away when you was happy here, and I sware I never helped him. If things get bad at home write me a letter or tell Carrie Bean. I know theres laws about children and what you cant do to them and I reckon Mr Joseph here knows what to do. Sam sends love and love from me Aggie.*

To Carrie Bean she wrote,

> *Dear Mrs Bean, Please will you keep an eye out*
> *for Melia? I don't trust Dad to look after her*
> *proper, he might knock her about and all that. If*
> *you get worrit write to me here and this is the*
> *address. With love, Aggie Flack.*

She wrote the addresses neatly and took both letters to the Post Office.

Harvesting was now in full swing, with Mr Joseph and his farm man and boy, William and Tom, out all hours and coming in at odd times sweaty, sunburnt, and exhausted for drinks and snacks. Aggie seemed to be forever filling bottles of tea: cold, sweet tea swigged out of a bottle kept the harvesters going in the heavy heat.

In the midst of all this, Mr Joseph found time to do something about Melia, too. He went to talk to the vicar—that same vicar who had warned him that his maid-of-all-work was a witch.

The vicar, even taller than Mr Joseph, looked down his long beaky nose at him. 'This is the girl I talked to you about?' he demanded, not exactly friendly.

'No . . . no . . . her younger sister,' said Mr Joseph. 'She lodged with Mrs Minster and attended church with her.'

'Oh . . . young Amelia!' said the vicar, suddenly more sympathetic. 'A pretty little puss. And you think she's in danger? From her father?' He raised his eyebrows. They came down slowly as Mr Willett talked on.

'So you think the mother's was a suspicious death,' the vicar said finally, stroking his chin.

'I've no evidence,' said Mr Willett. 'Aggie thinks so—and she was there, much of the time. Her young brother thinks so—a sharp lad. The doctor in that village is worse than useless, and ought to be struck off. I don't know where Melia will turn for help if she is ill-treated; probably not to her sister, as you know. A word from you to the vicar there, just to alert him to the situation, might be a godsend.'

'Yes,' said the vicar meditatively, 'yes, I'll do that. Yes, tonight. And how's the chapel?' He gave Mr Joseph an amused, indulgent smile; to him, chapel people were wasting their time and God's but, poor things, they knew no better. You had to treat them as human, even if they had no idea what real religion was about.

When Mr Joseph had gone the vicar sat down, spread his gangly elbows across his desk, and wrote a long letter in flowery handwriting. It began, 'Such goings-on in your Deep Fens as I never heard of—prepare to be amazed!' and it ended: 'Your brother in Christ, Jno Custerson.'

The vicar in Little Needham was certainly amazed when he read it.

When Melia had been gone five weeks, on a Saturday morning, the last letter in this series came, for Aggie. It came during breakfast, and Aggie put it in her apron pocket to read later, when the twins and Grace had been fed and washed and she could draw breath. She read it standing at the kitchen sink, the washing-up piled in front of her.

The envelope was written in a sprawly, scrawly hand and the address was so inaccurate that Aggie was surprised the postman had understood it. But it was unmistakably Melia's writing. Aggie grabbed the letter open and spread it out. The page was badly scribbled, and splashed, but the meaning plain enough.

> *Dear Aggie*, it said. *Please come and get me out of here—its horible its all work and Dad hits me. Please come I never ment all what I said and Im real frit Aggie do come. Melia.*

'Is it from your sister?' asked Mrs Ruth, coming up behind Aggie.

144

'Yes, and it's nothing like her! All blotty and badly spelled, and she's a good writer and can spell lovely,' said Aggie. She stuffed the letter back in her pocket. 'I'll look at it later on, and Sam can see it,' she said. 'I won't think about it now. This water's getting cold.'

Sam's overnight visits were arranged for every month, and another one was due that night. Sam rode up in the early afternoon, as on Saturdays his work ended at half-past twelve. Aggie heard the clatter of his bike in the yard and ran out to him.

'Come up to me attic, Sam!' she said urgently, and Sam trailed upstairs after her.

'Cor, Aggie!' he said. 'I'm that hot. Give me some water, if you've got it in your jug.'

'Read that while I pour it,' said Aggie. Sam puzzled his way through the letter, swallowing water down as soon as Aggie put a glass in his hand.

'She sounds desperate,' said Aggie. 'And look at them splashes on the page. I reckon she cried over it, Sam.'

'No, she never,' said Sam. 'Them splashes go sort of sideways; tears fall down splosh. That looks like she got her fingers wet and flicked water over it.'

'She could still be desperate,' said Aggie. 'You know Melia. She'd act a deathbed scene if she were really dying.'

'And if she weren't dying, too,' said Sam. 'Don't take it too hard. Show it your Mr Joseph when he comes in. Reckon he wants some help, up in the barley field?'

'Likely,' said Aggie. 'I'll get me hat.'

The two young Flacks spent a cheerful afternoon helping with the harvest. One or two of the village boys were helping, too, and the hard work and the jokes put Melia and her woes out of Aggie's head. She and Sam plodded back to the farm when exhaustion hit them, ate a huge supper, and went up to bed. Mr Joseph was still out in the field, making the best of a brightly moonlit night, and Melia's letter was still in Aggie's pocket.

Lightning woke Aggie out of a profound sleep. There was no thunder and no rain: only brilliant flashes jagging down like upside-down trees to the earth. Aggie got up to look. The moon was free of the cloud and the combination of moonlight and flashlight was a wonder.

Aggie poured out some water into her bowl, to wash her sticky arms and face. As she bent over it she saw, in the light of another flash, not herself but Dad and Melia. Dad was shaking Melia by the shoulders, his face a mask of fury, and Melia was cowering away from him. 'Aggie, do come,' her sister's voice seemed to say to her.

THIRTY-TWO

Aggie shook Sam awake most ungently, bumping his head against his thin pillow when rocking his shoulders failed to rouse him.

'Blast it!' yelled Sam, pushing himself up on his elbows. 'What the devil are you at? You've near bust me brains out!'

'Shut up!' hissed Aggie. 'Don't holler. Sam, we got to go to Dad's; something's up between him and Melia.'

'Well, we know that,' said Sam reasonably. 'That were in her letter.'

'Something else,' said Aggie. 'I seen him with her; he were half killing her and she . . . she's terrified out of her wits.'

'What, Melia?' scoffed Sam. 'She don't scare easy. Where did you see this, anyway?'

'In me washbasin,' said Aggie. 'It felt like that were happening now. I'm going to go there; I can't not.'

'What, now?' said Sam. 'It's the middle of the night, and a storm's on. Wait till the morning, and tell your Mr Joseph. If Dad's beating Melia it'll take more than you to stop him.'

'She's so alone there,' said Aggie. 'Who'd she ask for help, Sam? Who'd she tell?'

'She wouldn't, would she?' said Sam. 'She'd be trapped. But how do you think you'd stop him? You never could.'

'If he thought I'd tell the village—if he thought the Rough Music would come round—that'd stop him,' said Aggie.

'So it would. Might, anyway,' said Sam. 'How do you reckon on getting there?'

'Borrow your bike,' said Aggie. 'Can I? I can't ride proper, but I could scoot.'

'You wouldn't get far,' said Sam. 'Anyway, I'm coming with you.'

The two went soft-footed down two lots of stairs, climbed out of the parlour window and put their boots on out of doors. Sam's bicycle was leaning by the house wall; they got it out of the gates and launched it into the silent, empty street. They started off, with Aggie sitting on the crossbar and Sam pedalling. It was an uncomfortable business, and the bike wobbled and swerved. They struggled on, with breaks while one ran and the other 'scooted' when Sam got tired of pedalling. It was slow progress, especially after the moon went into cloud and they had to pick their way through thick darkness. When they were near one of the many drainage channels, Aggie insisted that they walked; she had not forgotten her winter journey and the fear of death by drowning.

Twice they had to shelter from sudden downpours. The first time, near Frog End, they got quickly into a barn and kept reasonably dry; the second time there were only trees at hand, and Sam dived under a leafy chestnut, bike, Aggie, and all.

'Cor blast!' exclaimed Aggie, sliding off the bike. 'Don't you know no better than to shelter under a tree? Come out, you daft gowk; you'll be a goner if that's struck. Trees are deadly in storms.'

'That's all the shelter there is,' said Sam. 'I'm stopping.'

He crouched near the trunk of the tree, pulling his cap well down. Aggie had no hat, having left in too much of a hurry to think of one; but she guessed that Sam's stripy muffler would be in his bicycle basket, fished it out, and wound it around her head. It was a prized possession of Sam's, knitted for him by Sister Flo, and he seldom left it behind. She huddled against a tall hedge, but it gave her little protection. When the rain slacked off and the moon reappeared to light the road, Aggie was soaked and Sam not a great deal better.

It was seven miles from Hardingley to Marksey, and another seven from Marksey to Little Needham. By the time they were through the town both Sam and Aggie were aching with tiredness and strain. But they forced themselves to go on, counting down the remaining distance from each familiar landmark.

By the time they got to Dad's cottage there was a gleam of daylight in the sky, and the moon's brightness was fading. By this weird mixture of light they saw, as they drew close to the cottage, that smoke was seeping thickly from the downstairs window and from around the frame of the door.

THIRTY-THREE

'House is afire. What'll we do?' shouted Aggie, flinging down the bike.

'That may not have got a real hold yet,' said Sam. 'Stand back! I'll inch the door open and get a look inside.'

As the door opened a little, smoke came out in a stinking cloud and a red glow showed. Sam took a sideways step inside and almost at once shot out. His face in the half-light looked ghastly; his eyes stared. He spun around and was heartily sick into the currant bushes.

'What's up? What's in there?' cried Aggie, catching his terror.

'Dad's dead. He's in there. Shot,' gasped Sam. 'I can't go in again. I can't.'

'All right, Sam,' said Aggie. 'I know you can't.' She did indeed know of the horror death held for Sam: he had run away howling, poor little lad, at the sight of Bowleses' drowned baby.

'I'll go in,' she said. 'Melia's in there, for sure. If only I knew where!'

Her eyes fell, as she spoke, on a puddle in the cottage pathway, glinting in the eerie light. As Sam was sick again, Aggie crouched over the puddle and muttered towards it, 'If that's God as sends me seeings, or whoever that is if it ain't, send me one now. I never asked before and I'll never ask again. Show me Melia.'

Under her eyes, as they lost focus, the rainwater seemed to shiver and the dark shape which was her own reflection to dissolve; and just for a moment she saw her own old bedroom, a rumpled bed, and under it the half-hidden shape of a small huddled body.

As her sight cleared she jumped to her feet, wrapping the still-wet muffler around her face. 'I'm going in!' she shouted to Sam, through the wool; and sidled through the house door, pulling it shut behind her.

And she saw what Sam had seen: her father, his head a bloody mess; the shotgun fallen on the floor at his side; and Piper, neatly shot through the brain, lying dead on the other side of him. The hearthrug was in flames, and the skirting-board beyond it, and one of Dad's trouser legs was beginning to smoulder.

Aggie didn't stay to look twice, but pushed through the door at the bottom of the stairs and fought her way on up through the choking smoke.

In the bedrooms, the smoke was not so thick; and in what had been the children's room Aggie peeled the scarf off her face and called softly to Melia.

'Mely!' she said. 'It's Aggie. You wrote me, and I'm come. Come on out, me love; that's all all right now.'

From under the bed Aggie heard Melia whimper, but not with words. Aggie crawled to her, felt, and found a hand—as cold as death and gripped into a fist.

'Come on, me love,' urged Aggie.

'Aggie!' whispered Melia. 'Dad . . . Dad . . . '

'I know,' murmured Aggie. 'Dad's dead, Melia. I reckon he shot himself; but anyway, he's dead. You'd best come out, little 'un. Come along, duck.'

Melia's cold fist turned into a cold hand, clutching Aggie's. She unrolled from her bunched-up position and let Aggie tow her out from under the bed.

'Now we're getting out of here, Mely,' said Aggie. 'A peat's fell off the fire and set light to the rug, and it's all smoky below. We'd best look slippy and get ourselves out.'

'I won't go by him!' whispered Melia.

'Yes, you will. You just won't look,' said Aggie. 'You want something over your mouth and nose to stop the smoke. This'll do.'

She picked up what she thought was a towel from the foot of the bed, dipped it in the water jug and muffled Melia's face in it; she also re-damped Sam's scarf and covered her own face again.

Melia stumbled down the stairs after her, and stopped dead at the bottom as—of course—she looked at Dad. Aggie turned round, seized Melia under the arms in a tight hug, and backed—dragging Melia after her—to the door. She rammed it with her back and both girls half staggered, half fell into the fresh air and the growing light. They were both choking from the smoke, their eyes and noses running.

As soon as she could breathe well enough Melia began to cry, with the uninhibited howling of a very small child.

Sam was up and on his bicycle. 'Thank God you found her!' he said to Aggie. 'I'm off to Fitches'—I'll get help. Shall I tell them Dad's dead? Perhaps they won't come, if there's nobody to save.'

'They'll come,' said Aggie, dragging in a painful breath. 'They'll want to see the corpse.'

She turned back to Melia, and saw with a jolt of sorrowful memory that what she had wrapped around Melia's head was Mam's Paisley shawl.

Melia was crouched, her hands on the ground and her head sunk between her shoulders. She rocked backward and forward on her toes, lost in her shock. Aggie put a reassuring hand on her shoulder, but Melia shook it off violently.

'Don't!' she shouted. 'Don't! I don't want you, witchy. I want me mam. I want her. You witched her dead, didn't you? Witch her back, then.' Her cry turned almost to pleading. 'Witch her back, Aggie. You can.'

This was too much for Aggie. She hauled Melia to her feet and shook her fiercely, yelling out, 'I can't. I never. I want her too; I'd give anything if she was here. I can't raise her. If I could, I would—even though I'd go to hell for it and burn for ever.'

She let go of Melia suddenly. Melia's noisy words had turned to screams of terror; her face was fixed in a mask of sheer fright. She was looking not at Aggie but over Aggie's shoulder, at something between them and the cottage.

Words became part of Melia's screaming. 'You done it! You raised her!' She shook, and beat at Aggie with her fists.

Aggie turned slowly, afraid. Silhouetted against the growing glare of the fire was a tall woman, moving towards them. Mam's height, Mam's figure.

Melia's fists hammered on Aggie's back. 'It's a haunt!' she screeched. 'You witch, Aggie! You done it to frit me.'

Horror came upon Aggie. She had said she would raise her dead mother if she could, in the teeth of hell. Was it possible she had done it?

'Please, God, save me,' she whispered. 'Help me, now . . .'

She thought she heard a voice—but whose?—call, 'Aggie! Come on.'

She stumbled towards the tall woman until she was near enough to see. The pale face was Mam's, but thinner; the bony hands—skeletal, almost—were Mam's, except for their extreme fragility.

Light flared as flames burst through the window of the cottage.

'Mam,' said Aggie hesitantly. 'Mam!' She took another step. 'You was buried.'

'Not me, no,' said the woman. 'That weren't me.' She held out her arms to Aggie, who rushed to hug her. As— even through the smoke—she smelt the remembered salty sweetness of her mother's skin, and the musk of her hair, Aggie's doubts dissolved into a rush of tears.

'Let me go now,' said Mam gently, after they had clung and rocked together for minutes—or seconds? 'I must see to the child.'

Melia was silent now, standing stiff and staring. Mam moved to her with slow steps and put a hand lightly on her head, stroking the tangled hair.

'That's me, Mely,' she said, 'not a haunt. You fair do talk some nonsense. What I heard you saying—you know better yourself. Give me a kiss, now.'

Melia hung round Mam's waist, beyond words. 'Am I dead, too?' she asked at last. Mam's laugh told her otherwise.

There was a sudden outburst of noise—voices, calling; and running feet. Ahead of the hurrying men came Sam, leaping off his bicycle. Even in the uncertain light he knew Mam at once. He did what no Flack had ever done and fainted, going down, as Aggie told him afterwards, like a sack of potatoes.

There were Bob Fitch and his elder brother Ted, and their brawny father, with trousers pulled on over their nightshirts. The noise they made passing his house had waked Mr Bowles, and he arrived almost simultaneously. He brought two buckets and the Fitches brought three, and a human chain was made from pump to cottage, Aggie being one of the links. By the time day was definitely day, and not the remains of night, the fire was out and the cottage still standing—smoke-blackened and reeking, but saved.

In all the rush of activity Aggie still had time to observe that the Fitches, and Mr Bowles, were not astonished to see her mother. They greeted her kindly and Mr Bowles warned her not to get cold.

'Fire's out, Mary,' he said to her at last. 'You and the young ones should get inside and get some rest.'

The everyday world came back to Aggie in a jump. 'Morning, ain't it!' she said. 'I got to get word to my master where I am; I came off without leave, last night.'

'Coroner should be told, too,' said Mr Fitch.

It was settled that Mr Fitch should go to the local police and that Ted, who wanted to exercise a young horse, should ride to Hardingley.

'Go quick, then, Ted,' said Aggie. 'Sunday. You'll need to get there before Mr Joseph goes to chapel.'

Ted winked and went off whistling.

'Come on, then, children,' said Mam, who had one arm round Melia and one around Sam, who still felt weak. 'Let's go in.'

Aggie looked at the damp and stinking cottage, and back at Mam.

Mam laughed. 'Not there,' she said. 'We needn't ever go back there. Landlord can have that back, and welcome to it. Where I've been living—we'll go there.'

'Bowleses'?' asked Aggie.

'Old Matty's,' said Mam. 'That's where I've been.'

THIRTY-FOUR

'Witch-house!' moaned Melia and would have pulled away from Mam if Mam had not held her firmly.

Matty Abbs was up and busy, boiling eggs at her open fire. Bread and milk stood on her table, and among the crockery a tall lamp was lit—one with a silver stand twisted like barley sugar. Aggie's eyes fastened on this.

'Oh, Mam!' she exclaimed. 'If I'd remembered where I'd seen this lamp, I'd have known you was still alive.'

Mam, who now looked whitey-yellow with exhaustion, sank down in a high-backed chair; but she still had the strength to smile at Aggie.

'That lamp's been a friend to me,' she said. 'If Matty stood that in her window, I'd know to sneak over, when I could. I got letters sent here from your Aunt Jane. Your dad never knew.'

'So you crept off here and hid, when they thought you was dying?' demanded Aggie.

'Best place for a hideout, ain't it?' said Matty Abbs, bringing the eggs to the table. 'Whoever visits the witch's house? Nobody comes that ain't desperate.'

The warmth had revived Sam. 'Bowleses knew you was here, Mam,' he said. 'Fitches, too.'

'They're near neighbours,' said Mam. 'They couldn't help knowing. They can keep a secret. And I got Lilian Bowles to tell Carrie. Nobody else knew. I didn't dare show me face, for fear of your dad; and I didn't dare let any of you know, for fear he got at you. And I'm talking no more, for now. We'll hear Melia's story.'

'He beat me, Mam,' said Melia. 'I'm all over bruises. He kept on, but last night were worst. I thought he'd kill me, and I ran off upstairs. I was afraid he'd come after me, but he never. Then the Rough Music came.'

'What, to our house? Did they know about you and Dad, then?' demanded Aggie.

'No, it were about Mam,' said Melia. 'I'd never heard that before. They were banging on saucepans and kettles and tin trays and such, and shouting out all in rhythm; it were real creepy. I looked out but I couldn't see who that were, except they were men or men and boys.'

'What did they shout?' asked Sam, fascinated.

'I couldn't hear all of it, because of the banging,' said Melia. 'It were something like—

> "Noah Flack! Noah Flack!
> Where's your wife?
> What did your old girl die of?"

'Then every so often all the banging stopped and they all shouted out,

> "Clear out! Clear out!
> Noah Flack—don't come back!"'

'I can make better poetry than that,' said Aggie. 'Did they bang at the door?'

'Not so's I heard,' said Melia. 'After a bit, they went away. Then I heard the gun; that went off twice.'

'What did you think?' asked Mam.

'Thought he'd kill me,' said Melia. 'I hid under the bed.'

'It were Piper he killed,' said Sam. 'Poor Piper.'

'Is that it, then?' asked Matty Abbs. 'No sorrow but for the little old dog?'

'Who'd cry over Dad?' retorted Melia.

Aggie did sigh a little. Not because she would miss Dad, but because of the fact that nobody would.

'Main thing is, we got you back,' said Sam to his mother. 'How come you was at the fire? Did you smell burning?'

'Matty did, and she called me,' said Mam. 'I snatched up a coat to put over me nightgown, and I came running. I thought Melia were in there.'

'I ran too, till I saw Melia were out,' said Matty Abbs. 'You did a good job there, Aggie Flack.'

'What roused up the Rough Music to come to Dad, Mrs Abbs?' asked Aggie, when breakfast had been eaten and tea was being drunk. 'People thought Mam were dead. What made them suddenly wonder, "What did Mary Flack die of?" '

'There's been talk,' said Matty Abbs. 'Vicar started it.'

'Vicar!' exclaimed Aggie and Sam.

'He went for the churchwardens and asked about your mam's death, and talked about digging her up again,' said Mrs Abbs. 'Then he got on to Dr Mortlock, and Dr Mortlock he swore on the Bible that she died of typhus and nothing more. So vicar said that should all be dropped and forgotten. But once talk's begun, it won't just stop. Most people wouldn't think too much of Dr Mortlock's Bible oath; and anyway, were he in his right mind when he saw the corpse?'

'Is he ever?' said Aggie bitterly. 'But that makes you think, don't it, Mam? If Dad could claim he'd done nothing wrong, and say you'd died of typhus, why wouldn't he open the door of the house last night and face them out?'

'Ah . . . why?' said Mam. 'He were always frit of people, your dad. He might act rough but he were deep-down scared.'

'I still don't see why he shot Piper,' said Sam.

'He loved Piper, like he didn't love us,' said Aggie. 'He'd be afraid Piper wouldn't be looked after, and would pine for him.'

'He didn't worry I mightn't be looked after,' said Melia sharply.

'Well, you will be,' said Aggie. 'Mam's here.'

In the pause in the conversation which followed, hoofbeats were heard; and in a moment Ted Fitch was standing as near the cottage door as he dared come. Aggie hurried to open it.

'Did you see Mr Willett?' she demanded.

'I did that,' said Ted. 'He's driving over after chapel, and he'll take you all back with him. Your mam, too, if she'll go.'

'I'll go,' said Mam.

THIRTY-FIVE

Even on Monday, there was no talk of Mam's going back to Little Needham. Instead, Mrs Ruth had a bright idea.

'You're a needlewoman, Mrs Flack,' she said, 'and here's a house full of needlework to be done. I've got cloth, but I've got no time; and there's curtains to be made, and dresses even—Aggie could do with new things for the autumn, and so could Flora and Grace. If you were able to stay a week, now, you and Aggie could spend some time together, and Melia could come in after school.'

It was an interval of calm for Aggie. Sam was back at Brother Ernie's and at his work at Matthews, and Melia was back at Mrs Minster's, rapturously received. Melia behaved to Aggie with nothing worse than sisterly scratchiness, and there seemed to be no more talk of witchcraft going round. People in the village spoke to Aggie, though some were a little guarded. They all at least managed, 'Sorry about your dad—glad about your mam,' and Aggie felt this was a start.

She did feel she needed to talk to Mr Joseph about what had happened, and did this in the farm kitchen. It was an odd set-up for a serious talk. Mr Joseph had brought in a sick hen and, with the bird tucked under his arm, was bathing its feet in disinfectant.

'There's something I ought to tell you, Mr Joseph,' Aggie said awkwardly.

'About your father's death?' said Mr Joseph. 'Come to that, Aggie, there's a question I'd like to ask you. How come that you and Sam took off like that in the middle of the night, and didn't wake me and tell me what was going on?'

'You're not silly. I reckon you can guess the answer,' said Aggie. 'That were a seeing, and what I saw made me sure things weren't right between Dad and Melia. He were knocking her about and I didn't know but what he might kill her.'

'I see,' said Mr Joseph. 'But you could have trusted me, you know.'

'Something like that, that's a family matter,' said Aggie, at her most stubborn. 'And about Melia, Mr Joseph. Who's paying for her at Mrs Minster's? Is it you? Mam wants to know.'

'I pay a bit,' said Mr Joseph. 'It is only a bit. Mrs Minster's glad to have her, and just charges her keep.'

'That'll be paid back to you one day,' said Aggie. 'When I can manage it. And thank you, for now.'

'The Lord rewards,' said Mr Joseph, with a grin. 'What was it you were going to tell me?'

'It were understood between us that I'd never ask for a seeing,' said Aggie. 'But I did. When we got to Dad's and there were smoke coming out of the house, I prayed to see where Melia were, so I could get her out quickish. I did see, too; in a puddle. It were God I prayed to, Mr Joseph.' At least, I think so, she added in her own thoughts.

'And was it a true seeing?' asked Mr Joseph.

'Yes; I found her straight off,' said Aggie. 'I wouldn't have done it, if I weren't desperate.'

'I see,' said Mr Joseph. 'I don't think it's a deadly sin, Aggie; but I hope you won't be desperate again.'

'I don't think I'll have any more seeings,' said Aggie. 'Things will be different now. I'm growed up.'

Somehow, Mrs Ruth contrived things so that Aggie was not too busy that week, and there were frequent occasions when Aggie, sometimes with Grace and the twins, could join Mam in her sewing-room. The big attic had been transformed for Mam's use, with a trestle table set up for her work and a comfortable chair by the window for the fine work that needed good light. Aggie—when not too occupied with the children—took out tacking stitches, sewed on buttons, darned in ends of thread, and kept the scissors out of small hands.

A lot of talking went on between Aggie and her mother, too. Aggie deeply relished these conversations by the sewing-room window and egged her mother on to tell every detail of her adventures.

'You ain't told me yet what made you decide to run for it,' she said during the first of their talks. 'What gave you the idea, Mam?'

'You saw yourself how ill I were,' said Mam. 'I ain't stupid, Aggie. When I add two and two I don't make five and a half; and I knew I were being poisoned. I reckoned your dad and that Lizzie Goose were adding something to me herb tea. I were always took worse when I'd had some of that.'

'And the calves'-foot jelly,' said Aggie. 'Were that poison too? Carrie Bean brought it, but I reckon Eliza Goose made it.'

'I'd wager so,' agreed Mam.

'So what did you do?' pestered Aggie. 'Mam, you should have told me. I'd have helped.'

'I thought it were best if I got out of it on me own—if I could,' said Mam. 'And I could. Remember I told you I weren't always asleep when they thought I were asleep? I acted worse than I were, the last day or so. I knew I'd got to get out of that house, and I saved me strength.'

'So when did you go?' asked Aggie.

'I heard them talking,' said Mam. 'From what they said, I reckoned they'd got me death certificate already. That Dr Mortlock would sign anything Lizzie Goose put in front of him. They were planning me funeral,

Aggie; and I thought it wouldn't be long before they sneaked upstairs and held a pillow over me face.'

'Oh, Mam!' breathed Aggie.

'Well, they didn't, did they,' said Mam. 'They made the mistake of going off to the pub—'

'I heard them!' exclaimed Aggie. 'I were outside. I wish I'd seen you.'

'I waited a while, then I took me money and a few clothes and I got out,' said Mam. 'Remember that spare key I had cut?'

'A mercy you did,' said Aggie. 'I can't get over the wickedness of them two. They broke the law, leave aside what they planned. There were a false sistificate—'

'Certificate,' said Mam.

'Well then,' said Aggie. 'Dr Mortlock wrote a lie and Dad and that Goose, they had a funeral. What for, when they knew you wasn't dead?'

Mam began to laugh. 'They'd got ahead of themselves,' she said. 'They were proper caught out. They'd got the death certificate, arranged the funeral, got the coffin made. Then all of a sudden they hadn't got no corpse. No more they couldn't say "Good news—she's better" because I weren't there. They wanted me out of the way so they could live together in that house, too. Simplest thing were to bury me.'

'Wonder what they buried,' mused Aggie.

'What were missing, when you went home?' asked Mam. 'How about me books?'

'Of course!' exclaimed Aggie. 'Your books had gone, and some of your clothes.'

'Ah—to wrap them round,' said Mam. 'Books tied in bundles, bundles tied together, and all that padded with clothes.'

'And prayers said over it!' said Aggie, and began to laugh. 'Oh, Mam, no wonder they nailed that coffin lid down quick and wouldn't let nobody see you!'

'What will you do about it?' Aggie asked Mam when her laughter had died down. 'The coffin, and all your stuff that's inside it?'

'Nothing,' said Mam. 'Talk travels; people will soon know that's a fake. If vicar wants that dug up, let him dig. Them books will be spoiled by the wet.'

'Will you go back to Little Needham?' asked Aggie.

'For the inquest,' said Mam. 'And the funeral. And there's people I want to thank, who were good to us. And one I'd like to look in the eye.'

'Lizzie Goose,' said Aggie. 'She ought to be in prison, and that doctor, too.'

'They'll get their deserts,' said Mam. 'People won't want Eliza for handywoman no more; and I doubt anyone will want to go to Dr Mortlock.'

'The Lord rewards,' said Aggie piously, and did not notice her mother's smile.

THIRTY-SIX

During the week Mam was at Hardingley, telegrams went back and forth between her and Aunt Jane. It was finally settled that Mam should go straight from the farm to Aunt Jane's home in Wisbech. Aunt Jane had a small business as a needlewoman, and more work on hand than one person could do; she said she would be glad to have a partner and that Mam would soon pay her way. She offered a home to the young ones too.

'What'll we do about that?' said Mam to Aggie. They were up in the attic, cut-out material spread on the table and Grace asleep in her cradle at Aggie's side. 'Sam and you are well enough where you are,' Mam went on. 'Ain't that right?'

'That's right,' said Aggie. 'Sam's happy with his job, and with the Shutters; and I'm happy here, where I'm a help to Mrs Ruth. But Melia? Melia and I are better apart.'

'I'll be taking Melia with me,' said Mam. 'She's had a hard time, with Dad. I knew a bit about what went on then—Matty Abbs were a look-out for me. I meant to step in, but I wanted to be strong before I done it: I needed to be able to stand up to your dad, if he went for me. Melia needs more school yet, and she needs me.'

'You mean because she ain't growed up, and me and Sam are?' asked Aggie.

'Partly,' said Mam. 'But it's her being what she is, too. You and Sam, you'll get on all right in the world, in spite of taking some knocks. You're warm-hearted people, and warm hearts find out warm hearts. Melia ain't like you two. Things were bad between me and Dad by the time she were born; she never heard kind words and laughter in the house when she were a babe.'

'Is Gran right that Melia's jealous of me?' asked Aggie. 'She says she thinks so.'

'Could be,' said Mam.

'Melia kept on letting on she were frit of me,' said Aggie. 'Calling me witch.'

'Melia's frit of herself,' said Mam, and her fingers stopped sewing. 'Think, Aggie. If anyone in our family will get Granny Flack's knowing, that'll be Melia. That comes out in girls; and she's a Flack, which you ain't— except by the name. She may say she's frit of you: she could be even more frit of herself.'

'Oh, Mam—poor Melia!' said Aggie. 'But she'll be with you, and you can help her.'

'Knowing, and meaning well by people, that's one thing,' said Mam. 'Knowing and meaning bad by people, that's another—and that's trouble. She needs somewhere like your chapel. We'll find somewhere, in Wisbech; when I've found her a school.'

'About me not being a Flack, Mam,' said Aggie. 'Gran told me about all that. I know about me dad. Did you love him—the real one?'

'Oh yes, I loved him,' said Mam. 'He were a cheat to me. He were a lovely man, though; tall, and dark like a gypsy, and a wonderful talker. If he walked through that door now, I'd go right up to him and kiss him; even knowing what I know.'

'Did he give you a brooch, with clasped hands?' asked Aggie. When Mam nodded she exclaimed in delight, 'I got that—bought it in the market! You must have it back, Mam.'

'You should keep that, Aggie,' said Mam. 'I must have dropped that when I did me disappearing act, and Lizzie Goose must have found it. You have it: it'll remind you you're me own gal, when you feel sour that Melia's with me and you ain't.'

'I won't feel sour, now,' said Aggie. 'I don't feel sour, and I don't feel frit. Nobody calls me witchy now, not even Melia.'

'There ain't things that worry you still?' asked Mam. 'Seeings, and such?'

'I don't think I'll get them no more,' said Aggie. 'And if I do, I'm not scared: I got prayers all round me, all the chapel's, keeping me safe. And that's funny—I don't make so many rhymes now, to jolly me along. Maybe that's because I'm happy here. Hope Farm's a good place to be.'

She went to pick up Grace, who was awake and beginning to grizzle, and Mam nodded.

'Learn all you can here,' said Mam. 'And copy how they talk, your master and mistress. They talk real nice.'

'They don't come from round here,' said Aggie, as Grace's hand gently patted her face. 'They were both schoolteachers once, till Mr Joseph come into some money and decided he'd try a farm.'

'Don't know if he were wise,' said Mam. 'That's all ups and downs, on a farm.'

'This harvest's an up,' said Aggie. 'Mr Joseph reckons I'll get ten pound as me share.'

'Ten pound!' exclaimed Mam, amazed. 'Ten pound's riches.'

'Even with ten pound, even if I learn a lot and talk proper, I'll still be little old Aggie Flack out of the Fens,' said Aggie.

'None the worse for that,' said Mam.

167

Other Oxford Fiction

Sweet Clarinet
James Riordan
Shortlisted for the 1998 Whitbread Children's Award
ISBN 0 19 275050 X

Billy thinks growing up in wartime is fun—falling bombs, fiery skies. That is, until a bomb falls on him.

From that moment on, Billy's life will never be the same again. Horribly burned, Billy longs for death—but the precious gift he receives might just give him something to live for . . . and some hope for the future.

*'A **really** good book'*

Whitbread Judges

The School That Went On Strike
Pamela Scobie
ISBN 0 19 275051 8

'What can you do? Nobody listens to children.'
'Oh, no? Then we'll MAKE them listen! If the grown-ups won't go on strike—WE WILL!'

And that's exactly what Violet and the rest of the pupils at Burston School do. They are fed up with the way their teachers have been treated and decide that there is only one way to make themselves heard . . .

Based on true events, this is the story of a group of children who come together to fight for goodness and justice—it's the story of the school that went on strike.

The Throttlepenny Murder
Roger Green
ISBN 0 19 275052 6

Jessie hated old Throttlepenny, her mean-spirited boss. She spent her days dreaming of ways to hurt him, but she'd never have the nerve to turn her dreams into reality.

But Throttlepenny is murdered. It's Jessie that the police come for, and Jessie that winds up in jail. Will someone prove her innocence—before she's hanged?

Flambards
K. M. Peyton
ISBN 0 19 275024 0

Twelve-year-old Christina is sent to live in a decaying old mansion with her fierce uncle and his two sons. She soon discovers a passion for horses and riding, but she has to become part of a strange family. This brooding household is divided by emotional undercurrents and cruelty . . .

Chartbreak
Gillian Cross
ISBN 0 19 275043 7

When Janis Finch storms out of a family row, it starts a chain of events which transforms her whole life. For it's in the motorway café, minutes later, that she meets the unknown rock band, Kelp, who talk her into coming to their gig that night.

Janis goes along for the ride, and finds herself increasingly provoked by Christie, Kelp's arrogant lead singer. He pushes her into singing with them, and winds her up into a fever of rage, awe, and attraction. So when Christie asks her to join the band, Janis feels powerless to refuse—and her life explodes.

Against the Day
Michael Cronin
ISBN 0 19 275039 9

It is 1940. The Nazis have invaded, and Britain is now part of the Third Reich. All over the country, German military authorities are taking control, led by the brutal Gestapo.

But slowly, surely, a resistance is building throughout the land. A secret network of people are plotting to overthrow the Nazis and win back their freedom, at any cost. Frank and Les, two schoolboys, never meant to get involved—but find themselves part of a dangerous undercover operation that can only end in bloodshed . . .

Chandra
Frances Mary Hendry
ISBN 0 19 275058 5
Winner of the Writer's Guild Award and the Lancashire Book Award

Chandra can't believe her luck. The boy her parents have chosen for her to marry seems to be modern and open-minded. She's sure they will have a wonderful life together. So once they are married she travels out to the desert to live with him and his family—only when she gets there, things are not as she imagined.

Alone in her darkened room she tries to keep her strength and her identity. She is Chandra and she won't let it be forgotten.

River Boy
Tim Bowler
ISBN 0 19 275035 6
Winner of the Carnegie Medal

Standing at the top of the fall, framed against the sky, was the figure of a boy. At least, it looked like a boy, though he was quite tall and it was hard to make out his features against the glare of the sun. She watched and waited, uncertain what to do, and whether she had been seen.

When Jess's grandfather has a serious heart attack, surely their planned trip to his boyhood home will have to be cancelled? But Grandpa insists on going so that he can finish his final painting, 'River Boy'. As Jess helps her ailing grandfather with his work, she becomes entranced by the scene he is painting. And then she becomes aware of a strange presence in the river, the figure of a boy, asking her for help and issuing a challenge that will stretch her swimming talents to the limits. But can she take up the challenge before it is too late for Grandpa . . . and the River Boy?

It's My Life
Michael Harrison
ISBN 0 19 275042 9

As soon as he opens his front door, Martin feels that something's wrong. But he never expects the hand over his mouth, the rope around his wrists, and the mysterious man who's after a large ransom. Before Martin knows it, he's a pawn in a dangerous game that becomes more and more terrifying with every turn . . .